SAVAGE LOVE

ELLA MILES

FREE BOOKS

<u>EllaMiles.com/freebooks</u>

Want to get my full length romance *Not Sorry* for **free**?

Want to get my **free** bonus novella—***Aligned: Ever After?***

Want to know when I put my books on sale for **free or 99 cents**?

You can get all of the above and more goodies here:
EllaMiles.com/freebooks

MY HEART FLUTTERS in my chest as Mark leans against the locker next to mine with a grin on his face. I try to focus on putting my books into my locker and packing up my backpack to go home, but I can't focus. I have a feeling I know what he's here to ask me and an unsettling feeling pulls at my stomach every second that passes.

"I have a question I'd like to ask you," Mark says.

I grin as I pile the rest of the books into my locker, not bothering to organize them at all. I turn to give him my full attention. "Ask away." Please don't let it be that he wants to invite me over to study for geometry again. I loved spending time with him the last time, but I want to be more than just his tutor.

He glances down as he rubs his neck.

I sigh. Mark is great. He plays soccer, he gets good grades, he's good looking. He's not exactly in the popular crowd, but he is definitely high on the social ladder. And every sign points to him being interested in me.

"How did your geometry test go?" I ask, breaking the awkward silence.

"Good, thanks to you."

"Have any plans for this weekend?" I ask at the same time he asks, "Will you go to prom with me?"

I stop breathing and my cheeks flush. He asked me. He finally asked me.

He smiles at my reaction. "So will you?"

I open my mouth to say yes, when my brother, Logan, walks up between us and his jerk of a friend, Carter, throws his arm over my shoulder.

"You ready to go?" Logan asks, looking from me to Mark.

"Can you give us a minute?" I ask glaring at my brother to leave me alone for five minutes so that I can say yes without having to be teased about it the rest of the night.

"Can't do that. We have to get home, have a busy afternoon planned," Carter says, staring at Mark as he pulls me tighter into his chest. I don't know why he's acting like this. He loves to tease me and torture me, but he's not interested in me. I can tell from the way that Mark is looking at him and then to me that he thinks we are together. We aren't.

"I should go. I have practice. I'll catch you later Victoria," Mark says, turning around and jogging quickly in the opposite direction.

"Mark wait," I shout as I run after him, but Logan steps in front of me blocking my path and Mark doesn't turn around or hesitate for a second.

"What are you doing?" I ask, crossing my arms over my chest.

"Mark Wagner really? You want to date Mark Wagner? You do realize that guy has slept with half of the girls in this school and that all he wants to do is get in your pants," Logan says.

I frown. "So? Maybe I want to sleep with him."

"No, you don't," Carter says from behind me.

I turn and glare at him too. "You guys can't tell me who I can and can't date."

Logan sighs. "Come on, Carter promised his mom he'd be home early today to babysit the new foster kids."

I grab my backpack off the hook and then slam my locker shut. I'll argue with Logan later once we drop off Carter. Once we are home and I'm alone I can call Mark to tell him yes.

"Here let me help you," Carter says grabbing my backpack out of my hands.

He swings my backpack over his shoulder along with his own as all three of us start walking down the hallway toward the parking lot where Logan's 1994 Buick LeSabre sits.

I raise an eyebrow at Carter not understanding at all why he's offering to carry my backpack. That is something nice people do or boys do when they are dating someone. It's not something that Carter does.

"I can carry my own bag, thanks," I say reaching out to grab my backpack back but Carter grips it tighter.

I exhale deeply and give up. It's not worth the fight anyway. I'm just glad that he's going to be at home tonight instead of over at our house like usual. I could use a break from him.

We get to the Buick, Logan climbs into the driver's seat while Carter opens the back door for me. I climb in giving him an *what the hell has gotten into you* stare. He hands me my backpack before closing the door and climbing in the front seat. Logan puts the key in the ignition and we all cross our fingers while we wait for the engine to purr to life. When it does, we all sigh in relief that we don't have to spend the afternoon walking the five miles home.

Carter turns the radio on to some hip-hop station. Neither Logan nor I like hip hop but it helps Carter relax, which is what he's going to need if he's going to survive an entire night at home. We all sit in relative silence, the music the only thing keeping us company until Logan pulls up in front of Carter's trailer and turns the car off. Carter stares at the front door, but doesn't move to jump out.

Our home life isn't great, but Carter's is far, far worse. He became a foster child when he was six. His foster parents have basically treated him as free labor and a welfare check ever since. He rarely stays at home, usually sleeping on our couch or in Logan's bedroom. Today is one of the rare occasions when he's required to be home. He's supposed to babysit his foster siblings.

Carter exchanges a glance with Logan and then opens the door and climbs out of the car. He doesn't say anything and we don't either. We don't say good luck dodging his foster father's beatings. We don't say keep your cool while the people that are supposed to be your parents throw all their money away on the slots instead of providing food and clothes for you. We don't say anything because despite not having to worry about getting beat, our life isn't much better. So we just watch Carter walk up to the door and disappear inside.

Logan doesn't start the car up again. Instead, we just sit outside and hope that Carter comes back. Even I, who hates Carter's guts and wishes I had some time to myself without having to worry about what stupid pranks he and my brother are going to pull on me, would rather have him here than getting beat.

"Why did you and Carter try to get between me and Mark?" I ask as I climb into the front seat.

"You're too young to date," Logan says ignoring me and staring at the door. He seems more worried than usual about his friend.

"I'm fifteen! That's plenty old enough. You started dating way before that."

"Yea and I shouldn't have. You don't want to end up like Amber, do you?"

I frown. "I'm not stupid enough to get pregnant in high school like my sister did."

He finally looks at me. "You're not having sex or dating until you're in college."

"You can't tell me what to do. You're not my father. You're only two years older than me."

He sighs and runs his hand through his hair. We both realize that it's time to go. That Carter is stuck inside for the night and there is nothing we can do to protect him. Not tonight anyway.

"I can't tell you what to do. Date Mark if that's what you want. Just be careful, you're the only one of us that has a chance at breaking free of this shitty town."

I smile a little as I twist my frizzy hair around my finger and put my feet up on the dashboard.

Logan starts the car and begins speeding off toward our house. He glances in the rearview mirror and suddenly steps on the breaks.

"What the hell?" I say as my body is thrust forward and then back abruptly.

Logan continues to stare in the rearview mirror as his face goes white. I turn around scared to glance behind me when I see Carter running toward our car. He throws the backdoor open and jumps in. Logan immediately steps on the gas as soon as Carter is safely inside. I see Carter's face out of the corner of my eye. His eye and cheek is black and blue.

We don't ask questions. We don't have to. And Carter offers up no explanation of what happened. We just drive to our house and pretend that this isn't our life. That we are normal kids that don't have to worry about problems like this.

Logan parks the car in the driveway to our house. It isn't much, just a little over a thousand square feet in total. We don't have a garage and the lawn has never been taken care of so it is mostly weeds at this point. We walk up the sidewalk that has large cracks in it and throw open the front door that no one ever bothers to lock. It's not like there is anything worth stealing inside anyway.

We all head to the kitchen. We're starving and food is the only thing that will make Carter forget about what just happened. Logan throws open the fridge and finds it empty. He opens the freezer and finds one bag of peas which he hands to Carter. He puts it to his face.

"Mom! We are out of food," I yell as I walk into the living room.

I fold my arms across my chest when I find our mother in her usual position, passed out on the couch from drinking. She works the night shift at a convenience store and then spends her days drinking or smoking. I don't even know why we bother calling her Mom, it's not like she is one. We are basically on our own, always have been, always will be.

I walk over to her because I can't take her crap today. I shake her shoulder until she finally stirs enough that she opens her eyes.

"What?" she barks at me, her voice sharp with plenty of bite at being awoken from her drunken state.

"We are out of food. And I need money to buy a prom dress." I know Logan and Carter are listening to me from the kitchen, but I don't care. I know Logan is just trying to protect me, but he isn't actually protecting me. I can take care of myself. And Carter is just being his usual self. If he isn't happy, then no one should be happy.

Mom sighs and closes her eyes again. "Take the cash in my purse to buy some food for tonight. And you don't need a prom dress. No one has asked you."

"Mark Wagner asked me."

She half chuckles and half chokes on her saliva. "I didn't think any boy would ask out a girl as flat chested as you."

My head falls back and my eyes close tight trying to block out the disgusting woman in front of me. Her words mean nothing to me.

"What are we going to do about a dress?" I ask. I don't bother asking about getting my hair done or buying some half decent makeup for the occasion because I know the answer to that is a no.

She yawns. "Wear one of Amber's old ones or get a job and pay for one yourself."

My heart sinks. I only have a few days until prom. I won't have time to find a job, let alone make enough to afford a dress. And Amber was much curvier in high school than I am. Her old dresses will never fit me, not without some serious help.

I'm not going to let it deter me though. Good things don't happen to me very often. And I'm not going to let my brother, his best friend, or even my mother from preventing me from having a good time at prom like every other normal teenager.

I storm into the kitchen and find her purse lying on the kitchen counter. While Logan and Carter both stare at me, I reach into it hoping for a miracle that there is actually money in here.

I pull out the wallet, open it, and pull out the single bill that sits inside. A five dollar bill. It couldn't even be a twenty. With a twenty we could buy enough real food for us to last for days. Instead, we will have to settle on ramen noodles for the week.

I start walking out of the cramped kitchen and thrust the five dollar bill into Logan's hand as I walk by. He can go figure out what to do to prevent us from starving tonight. I can't deal right now.

I storm upstairs to my bedroom that I used to share with Amber. I throw open the sliding closet door that is barely hanging on. I start digging through the closet to the very back where I know Amber kept her prom dress. I pull out the single dress. It is light pink with some silver sparkles at the bodice. It's strapless and flows out at the waist. There is no way it will fit me. I have no boobs.

I walk over to the landline because we can't even afford cell phones. I dial Amber's number.

"Hey sis," she says.

"Hey, I need your help. A boy asked me to prom and I don't have anything to wear. Mom said I could wear your dress, but there is no way it will fit me."

"I'm sorry Victoria, I wish I could help." I hear the baby crying in the background and I know there is nothing she could do to help. She has much more important troubles.

"I shouldn't bother you with my stupid problems. How is Sailor doing?"

"She's fussy and misses her Aunt."

I smile. "I miss her too. I'll have to come visit soon."

We hang up and I realize what I already knew, but had to try anyway, that my sister can't even help me. If I want to go to prom with Mark, I'm going to have to figure it out myself.

I start removing my t-shirt and jeans. I might as well try on the dress and see what hope I have of making it fit by this weekend. When I'm down to my bra and underwear, I pull the dress up my body and zip up the back. I let go of the dress to walk to the bathroom and look at myself in the mirror but the dress instantly falls to the ground at my feet. I have no curves anywhere on my body to hold the dress up.

I sigh and reach down and pick up the dress holding it up to my body while I walk to the bathroom. I step inside, turning the light on as I see just how big the dress really is.

I grab all the tissue paper we have and start stuffing my bra, hoping that if I can stuff it enough and maybe pin it slightly in the back, I can get it to stay up.

I hear a chuckle and I freeze, realizing that I didn't shut the door. I was too focused on the dress.

"I don't think there is enough tissue paper in the world to make you have tits big enough to hold up that dress," Carter says as he leans on the doorframe.

I glare at him. "No one asked you."

He shrugs and steps inside the bathroom behind me. He grabs the back of the dress around my waist and pulls it tightly until the front is flush to my skin.

My breathing stops at his touch. His touch is not a feeling I'm used to. I feel an electricity tingling from my fingertips to my toes when he touches me.

"There, that's better," he says, his eyes devouring my body in the mirror.

I narrow my eyes and remind myself to breathe. *He doesn't like you*, I remind myself. *And I hate him.*

"Know how to sew?" I ask.

"Nope," he responds.

I exhale deeply.

"Put some clothes on and come to Logan's room," he says.

"Did you guys get dinner?"

He shrugs. "We got alcohol."

I turn and walk out of the bathroom, but not before Carter's hands crawl across my lower back, sending chills down my back. I shake my head as I walk to my bedroom. I don't know what is wrong with me right now, but I need to remind my body that he's the enemy. Even when he tries to be nice once or twice a year, it's only to make the pain that much worse when he eventually hurts me again.

I shut my bedroom door and then find my baggiest sweatpants and sweatshirt. A shield of sorts to keep Carter from hitting on me.

I step into Logan's tiny bedroom that barely fits his queen

sized bed. I find Logan lying back on the bed, while Carter is sitting on the floor leaning against the opposite wall. Both hold a beer in their hands.

"Here," Carter says, holding out a beer to me.

I walk to Carter while I look at Logan, waiting for him to say that I can't have the beer. He doesn't say anything though. I've had a few beers before, but I've never drank with Logan. He never lets me. I don't know why today is any different, but if we aren't going to get to eat then we might as well get drunk to pass the time.

I take the beer from Carter and watch as he pats the floor beside him. I take a seat next to him despite my better judgment.

Logan starts playing some music on his radio and we all just sit there listening to the music while thinking about our shitty lives. Logan finishes his beer and then gets up, leaving Carter and me alone. I don't know where Logan is going, but neither of us ask or care.

Carter downs his beer while I continue to sip mine. "Want another?" he asks.

I finish mine and then nod, handing him my empty can. He takes it from me and tosses them both in the corner of the room before grabbing two more cans from the box sitting on the floor at the foot of Logan's bed. He hands one to me as he takes a seat next to me again.

"So who are you taking to prom?" I ask. I'm sure he's going. Logan's going with Michelle, a girl he's been seeing recently. And Carter wouldn't miss an opportunity to get a girl in his bed, or more likely my bed, while I end up sleeping on the couch.

He shrugs. "Haven't decided yet."

I raise an eyebrow. "Every girl you asked so far has turned you down," I joke even though I know it isn't true. No girl in our high school would turn down Carter. He's far too good looking.

No one can resist his charming smile. When he wants someone, he gets them.

"Don't say yes to Mark," he says.

I frown. "Don't start that again."

He fingers trace across my forearm as tiny goosebumps raise up and down my arm.

I pull my arm away and try to change the subject.

"What are you going to tell your teachers tomorrow when you come in with a black eye?" I ask.

He shrugs. "I'll come up with something."

"I have some makeup you can use. It's not the best but it might help."

He looks at me as a slow smile creeps up his face. "Do your worst."

I jump up and run to my bedroom to grab my small bag of makeup before walking back to Logan's bedroom. I feel the strange flutters in my stomach again as I take a seat next to Carter again. Logan is back on the bed drinking another beer, and Carter sets his down next to him as he looks at me.

I pull out my concealer and foundation and begin applying it around his eyes over the red and purple bruise that has formed on his face. I try to focus on the bruise instead of on his eyes but it's difficult when he's staring at me so intently. I've never seen him look at me this way.

I swallow hard and put down the makeup brush. "There, much better."

He doesn't respond or ask to look at himself in the mirror. I'll have to apply more in the morning, but I think it will work well enough that most people won't notice.

He reaches forward and tucks a strand of hair behind my ear. My heart stops, along with my breathing, and every other cell in my body. I don't know what that was. But it felt like something I never expected to feel from him. It felt like he cared. Like adoration. Maybe even more.

"You're beautiful, Tori," he says so quietly that I'm not sure I even heard him say it.

But his words are what I play over and over in my head as I fall asleep. They are what I think about when I decide to wait to call Mark and tell him I'll go to prom with him. They are what make me think that Carter wants to go to prom with me.

———

My heart races in my chest as Logan drives the three of us to school the next morning. Butterflies flip in my stomach throughout the day, until they become giant piranhas eating up my insides with nerves as the day ends and I know that I will see Carter again.

He's driven me crazy my whole life, but deep down I've always felt something for him. I've always wished that when he was with the other girls, it was me he was kissing instead. I just never thought he would feel the same way about me. I never thought he would call me beautiful. I never thought he'd choose me.

I've been avoiding Mark all day, but as the school day comes to a close there's no way for me to avoid him. He walks up to my locker just like he did the day before. Except this time, he barely looks at me and doesn't smile at me when I look at him.

I bite my lip trying to decide what I should do. Mark is great. He's been nothing but nice to me, but Carter...Carter brings me alive like nothing I've ever felt before.

I glance past Mark, and see Carter walking down the hallway to me.

'No' he mouths to me while nodding toward Mark.

I know he wants me to tell Mark no. I'm just not sure why.

I look at Mark and say words I never thought I'd say to him, "I'm sorry Mark, someone else already asked me to prom."

"Oh, okay Victoria. I'll see you around then." His eyes widen a little and then he walks away in shock.

I smile brightly at Carter who is walking toward me. This is it. He's going to ask me now that I turned Mark down.

He keeps walking toward me when a blonde woman grabs onto his waist. He stops and smiles at her before he leans down and kisses her on the lips.

My mouth drops open at what I'm seeing. How could I be so stupid to think that Carter would ask me to prom?

I turn back to my locker to keep the tears from falling. I'll cry later in my room. Alone. But not here.

"Hey Tori, you ready to go?" Carter asks.

I nod as I close my locker and place my backpack over my shoulder. He doesn't offer to carry my backpack like he did yesterday. Instead, he holds onto her like he's been waiting his whole life for her.

"I'm Lily," the blonde says.

"Victoria, Logan's sister," I say.

She smiles. "That's so cool that you're gay. I've never met a gay woman before. Have you found a girl to go to prom with you?"

My eyes flutter at her words. "What?"

Carter takes over for her. "No, Victoria hasn't found a girl to take her to prom. Maybe next year."

He pulls her in and kisses her again right in front of me while my heart is breaking. Carter has done some messed up shit, but this might be the worst. I've suffered plenty of physical pain because of him. But never heartbreak like this.

And it's not over. I'm never going to find a boyfriend, let alone a date, the rest of my high school career. Carter made sure of that with his stupid rumor that he started. Even though it isn't true, the whole school will believe him over me.

I've felt plenty of pain in my life. But my brittle heart has never been so hurt by a man that I thought behind all the bullshit he actually cared about me. I was wrong. A man like Carter could never truly care about me, because he doesn't have a heart.

1

VICTORIA

Ten Years Later

"You're fired," my boss, Will, says.

My mouth falls open a little. He's got to be kidding. He can't fire me. I'm his best employee. The company wouldn't survive without me.

"This is a joke, right?"

Will gets up from his large oak desk and walks around to my side. He sits on the edge of his desk as he looks at me with sad eyes.

He's not joking. That much is clear.

"I wish I were joking."

He crosses his arms over his chest as he looks even more distressed. I don't care how he feels right now. He's the one who made the decision to fire me.

"Are you sure? I mean...I thought I was doing a good job here."

I thought I was doing the best job here. I've worked at the company less than a year, but I am already heading three different PR projects. When I take over a project, I live and breathe for my clients, making sure that no obstacle goes unnoticed. I'm completely prepared for every negative aspect of every situation and know exactly how to spin it in a positive light.

"You were, Victoria. It's really not about your job performance."

"Then, why am *I* getting fired?" My whole body shakes as I speak much too loudly for this office.

I glance behind me at the glass doors that look into Will's office. The office was built for transparency so that we could all feel close, like a family. I used to enjoy how open the office felt, how light and airy it was. But, now that I'm getting fired and the entire office is staring at me, I wish it looked more like a dungeon I could hide in.

Will rubs the back of his neck. "Because the company is struggling. Decisions that were made long before you came here have left the company failing. We have to lay someone off, it's the only way we can afford to keep running."

I nod. I understand the need for layoffs. "That still doesn't explain, why me? I bring in more income than most of your employees, combined."

Will smiles a little at me. "You do. You're terrific. But being as good as you are also comes with a price. You negotiated the highest salary. And you were our last hire. Those two things mean you are the first one out."

I bite my lip to keep from saying what I really want to say. I want to chew him out. I want to say that it doesn't even make sense to let me go if I'm the best. But I don't. I just keep my mouth shut. I learned long ago that saying what I want to say usually just makes things worse.

"I'm sorry, Victoria."

I glare up at him. He doesn't get to be sorry. He's the one who can't lead a competent team. He's the one who doesn't make enough money so that he doesn't have to fire his employees to keep the company afloat.

"Are we done then?" I snap. I can't be in here any longer.

When I was first hired, I thought all my dreams were coming true. I got my dream job, in my dream city. But, now, I know it was too good to be true.

"Yes."

I get up and turn to walk out.

"But just know, Victoria"—Will lowers his voice—"that this is really for your benefit. Unless a miracle happens, the company won't survive the year. When this company goes down in flames, you will already be working your way up the ladder at your next company."

I stop at the door and smirk. "You're an idiot, Will, because you just lost your last chance to save your company. Because I was that miracle. I would have stepped up and started working a hundred hours a week or more for the same pay to ensure that this company survived. I would have done anything because I believed in this company. I liked my coworkers. I loved my job. But, instead of reaching out for help, you're getting rid of the only shot you had left. But you're right about one thing. I will already be at a more successful company while your company is ripped apart and sold piece by piece to try to give something to your investors."

I push the glass door open and walk out with my head held high to my desk. I keep a large fake smile plastered on my face as I glide across the room, pretending like I just quit instead of getting fired. I gather my laptop and things into my briefcase. And then I walk out, like my life is fine.

But, instead, my world just fell apart. I don't even make it to my car before the tears drop. Tears I would never let anyone else ever see, but in the darkness of the parking garage, they descend.

This was the absolute worst day for me to get fired. I just bought a new house last week. There are still boxes everywhere. My sister, niece, and I haven't even fully moved in yet. Putting down the down payment practically emptied my savings. I need a new job and fast.

I hit the steering wheel over and over, trying to get my frustration and pain out. This is the third time I've been fired in five years. None of them were my fault. I'm good at fixing people's problems. Everyone's, except for mine.

———

By the time I get to the house, the house that I thought we would live in for years to come but is now threatened, I have lost the tears and returned the fake smile to my face. I won't let them know that I just got fired. I can't. I won't let them worry. Ever.

I open the door, and before I even get inside, I'm tackled by two dogs and my ten-year-old niece.

I laugh as we all fall to the floor while I try not to bump into any of the boxes that are piled high everywhere.

"You're home!" Sailor squeals. "I thought you weren't supposed to be home until five."

I tightly hug her, loving that the second she's in my arms, I feel ten times better—but ten times worse at the same time. I try to focus on the happy feeling of getting to spend more time with my niece today.

"I got my work done quickly so that I could come be with you this week."

"Yay! Does that mean we can go to the beach?" Sailor's little eyes light up as her blonde curls hang down around her cheeks.

I smile. I'm not sure I could ever tell her no. I'd do anything for her. I'll do everything I can to make sure that she is taken care of. This is her home now, and I will make sure it remains her home, including flipping burgers, waitressing, or serving coffee. Anything. Let's just hope I don't have to resort to that.

I'm a generally positive person. But I do know how long it took me to find my last position. Six months. I had been offered several jobs before the last one, but none of them paid enough. None gave me the flexibility that I needed.

I look back at Sailor. I'll figure it out though. I don't have six months to make something happen. I have about a month of savings. I can find a job that fast in the San Francisco area, no problem.

"Absolutely! Let's go see if your mom wants to go."

Sailor's face brightens. "Good. I'm tired of being cooped up in this house."

I laugh. "You've been cooped up for a total of four hours."

She shrugs. "But it was a long four hours!"

"Your mom upstairs?" I ask, already knowing the answer.

Sailor nods.

"Go get changed into your swimsuit, and I'll go see if your mom wants to go."

Sailor shoots up the stairs to her bedroom while I go check to see if my sister, Amber, is out of bed yet. I knock on the door before I slowly enter her bedroom. She's still in bed, like I expected.

I go over to the window and open the blinds.

"It's a beautiful day, Amber."

My sister groans and covers her head with the thick comforter. I want to be angry. I want to yell at my sister to get up and go take care of her daughter. To get a job. Or, at the very least, spend time with Sailor. But I know that would be the opposite of helpful. Tough love never works with Amber.

We are different like that. Amber needs soft encouragement while I need tough love.

Amber has gorgeous, long blonde hair, just like her daughter, while my auburn hair makes it so that you wouldn't even know that Amber and I were related from our looks.

"I'm taking Sailor to the beach. You up for joining us? We would really like that."

"No."

I take a deep breath, needing to remain calm.

"You sure, Amb? It's a beautiful day out. You don't have to swim if you don't want to. Just come enjoy the day with us."

"No."

I walk over to the bed and sit on the edge while I rub her back, trying to encourage her to come. But we've been through this before. She had postpartum depression after Sailor was born. And despite trying to get her help, she's never gotten better. Losing her job and apartment didn't help. She's at one of her lowest places. And there is not much I can do to help her when she is like this but make sure she is taking her medications and going to therapy while letting her know I'm here for her when she finally makes it through the fog.

"Do you need anything before I go?"

"No."

I lean down and kiss her on the cheek. I wish there were more I could do, but depression is hard to fight. It's not something I can fix, no matter how much I want to.

"I love you, sis," I say, getting up before getting ready and heading to the beach.

———

I could live my life at the beach and never get enough of it. Sailor is the same way. She was meant to live in the water. Sometimes, I wonder if she was meant to be my daughter instead of Amber's. But then she does something that reminds me completely of my sister, and I know she is hers. And, when

Amber is healthy, she makes an amazing mother. It's just hard when she is in one of her depressed places. Hard for her to keep a job, hard for her to take care of her daughter, hard for her to even get out of bed.

That's why I have to have a job. I have to take care of Sailor when Amber can't. That's what family does. We pick each other up and handle things when others can't take care of themselves. If only I could convince my mother and brother of that, then maybe it wouldn't fall on me all the time.

Who am I kidding? I like the responsibility. I like being in control of the family. I like taking care of them. I just hoped life would go my way for once in my damn life.

My phone buzzes, and I don't have to look at the screen to know who it is. My mother, who recently married a wealthy doctor and now thinks she is mother of the year. At least she doesn't get drunk as often anymore. I consider not answering. I don't want to tell her that I got fired, but I'm not the best liar. She will know. But, if I don't answer, she will just keep calling all day long until I finally do.

"Hello?" I answer, trying to sound chipper.

"What's wrong?" my mother asks.

I frown. "Nothing's wrong."

"I know you. Something is wrong."

"What did you call me for, Mom?"

"Is it your sister again? What did she do now? I told you it was a bad idea to buy a house for her and Sailor. You are a successful businesswoman. You should have a nice penthouse downtown. Not throw all of your money away on a house in the suburbs where it takes you an hour to drive to work every day."

"Amber's fine. And I wanted to buy the house. It's a good investment, and I like being close to Amber and Sailor."

"Boyfriend trouble then? You are too young to worry about

dating. You should just focus on your career. You're in your twenties. You'll have plenty of time for boys later."

I sigh. I wish it were boyfriend trouble. I haven't had a date since graduating from college. No one wants to take on a woman who spends all her time working or with her niece.

"No, it's not boyfriend trouble."

I can feel my mother's scowl on the other end of the phone.

"It has to be your sister then. I told you she would take you down. That—"

"I got fired."

There's a pause.

"That can't be. You're awesome at your job."

I sigh. "I know, but that's why they let me go. They couldn't afford to keep paying me what I'm worth."

"Well, it's their loss then. But it's actually perfect timing."

Ugh. I don't want to hear whatever nonsense my mother is going to say next. This isn't good timing. This is the worst timing. If they had fired me even six months from now, I wouldn't feel so lost. So desperate.

"Why is it good timing?"

"You remember Lily Taylor?"

"Yes."

How could I forget Lily? She was the most popular girl in school. Smart, beautiful. My brother was obsessed with her even though she dated his best friend and my archenemy, Carter Woods, for most of high school.

"Well, she is in need of a fixer."

I smile. "Really? And how do you know that?" I regret the words the second I ask.

"Cathy told Cindy who told Melissa. Have I told you about Melissa's botched Botox job yet? It looks hideous. I don't know what she was thinking or who she went to, but—"

"Mom, I don't care about Melissa. I care about Lily and why she needs good PR right now."

"Oh, sorry, sweetie. Lily was engaged to Phillip. But it turns out, she had been cheating on him the whole time."

"Why does that matter?"

"Because she's running for Senate. It wouldn't matter that much, but her law firm also just got accused of several immoral acts. I don't think she was directly involved, but it's not looking good for her. She's currently shopping for a good PR firm."

"There's just one problem. I don't run a PR firm."

My mother sighs. "So, start one. You can do anything you want sweetie. Go convince her to hire you. You know she will pay well, and if you can help her win, you'll have clients lining up for you."

I smile. She's right. I can fix my own problems by helping Lily fix hers. I just have to get to her quickly. Companies will be lining up for a chance to work for Lily Taylor.

2

CARTER

My mouth drops as I stare at the television screen, watching the mess unfold before my eyes. I've never seen anyone fall apart so completely, so quickly, and I'm in the crisis business. I've seen my fair share of meltdowns. In fact, I've created plenty of chaos before. But I never thought I would see Lily Taylor fuck up her whole life in a matter of seconds in a single interview. I just didn't think it was possible.

I've known Lily most of my life. She's smart and beautiful. Her family had money, and she went to the best schools. I even dated her for a year in high school. I was probably stupid for letting her go. I always knew that Lily was going to make something of herself someday. She could be anything she wanted. She had everything going for her. Intelligence, money, and good looks.

She's decided to go into politics. To become a senator and then make a presidential run.

But, from the look on Lily's face right now as she stares wide-eyed at the talk-show host, she thinks those dreams are squashed. Over. Gone.

And, if she were any other candidate, she would be. She

fucked up, and she knows it. But, lucky for her, I can fix all of her problems.

That's what I do. I fix people's problems and turn them into something amazing that works in their favor. I own a PR firm that only takes on the biggest problems with the highest-profile clients. Over the past five years, I have turned the company into the best PR firm in the country. No one does it better than Carter Woods.

But Lily is going to be a challenge. First, I'll have to convince her that her dreams haven't completely been destroyed. That she can still become a senator from North Carolina. And that I can get her there. But it comes with a price. I'm not cheap, but Lily can afford the best. If she really wants this, then she won't even bat an eyelash.

The interview is finally over, and I close the lid on my computer before picking up the phone.

"Ruby, can you come in here, please?"

"Be right there, Carter," my assistant answers.

A second later, Ruby bursts through my door with a large smile on her face. Her body is practically jumping up and down with excitement as she stands inside my office. She clasps her hands together to keep from exploding.

I raise an eyebrow at her. She's always a positive woman who is usually happy, but this is on a different level.

"Spill, Ruby," I say.

"You finally watched the Lily Taylor interview, didn't you?"

I nod, although I don't know why she says *finally*; it aired only a half hour earlier. And it doesn't explain her bubbliness.

She turns, ducking out of my office for a second, before returning with a thick file that she throws onto my desk. "This is everything I have on Lily Taylor. I cleared your schedule to make sure you have time to focus just on her for the next month. I have a flight for you this evening to Charlotte, North Carolina, and I booked a hotel room, although I'm sure you would rather stay with Logan. Just let me know, and I can cancel. I'm just so excited for you," Ruby squeals.

I narrow my eyes, not understanding why Ruby is so thrilled. "It will be a big account. If we succeed, we will have clients lining up, wanting to work with us, but I'm not sure why you are this enthusiastic about it, Ruby."

Her cheeks flush as she takes a step forward to my desk and begins flipping through the thick manila folder lying on top. She stops when she gets to a picture and points at it. My eyes drift down to the picture of Lily and me wearing our homecoming crowns after winning King and Queen. We were a perfect couple. If we had met later in life, maybe we would still be together, but we were far too young then for it to last.

I look back up at Ruby, who still has the goofiest smile I've ever seen on her face. "We used to date. So?"

"So? So, she is flawless. Just look at her! She's beautiful, smart, ambitious. She's your perfect match! This could turn into a romantic love story. You go save her reputation and career, all the while falling in love with your high school sweetheart. How awesome!" she squeals.

I look down at the picture of a woman I haven't thought about in years. She would be ideal for me. My career has always come first and will always come first. That's who I am. But, if I found a woman who was just as ambitious as I was, then maybe it would work. I would finally have a woman who understood me. Who wouldn't complain when I was at the office for far too long because she was, too. A woman who didn't care if we had kids. And, if we did, she'd agree that a nanny was the best person to raise them. Lily could be that person.

I smile, still holding the picture. "Thanks, Ruby."

She grins and leaves me alone. I grab my cell phone and call up Logan. He knows me better than anyone. He lives in Charlotte and won't have a problem with me crashing at his place. And he'll be the perfect wingman to help me get Lily.

————

I knock at the same time I throw the door open to Logan's apartment. I've been down a handful of times but not as much as I would like. North Carolina is a nice place to get away to when I need to relax, but I prefer the hustle and bustle of a big city like New York. And Logan is a bartender. Not exactly bringing in the big bucks, so he usually comes up to New York when he wants to have a good time.

"The fun has arrived!" I holler as I step into his apartment.

Logan gives me a bro hug when he sees me, slapping me hard on the back.

"I didn't expect to see you back here after last time," Logan says with a chuckle.

I frown, thinking about the last time I stayed here and how it took my chiropractor a month to fix my back after sleeping on his horrible futon. "I couldn't miss an opportunity to see you. But, if you haven't bought an actual bed for your guest room yet, then I'm turning around and getting you one right now. I'm not sleeping on that twenty-year-old futon again."

"Relax. My sisters already beat you to it and bought me a mattress for Christmas last year."

Images of Victoria and Amber pop into my head. Amber is older than Logan and me, and she wasn't around much. But Victoria...she was the annoying little sister that I never had. Logan and I loved torturing her. I haven't seen her in years, and the few times I've been back to see Logan, we have both been too drunk to talk about how his family is doing.

"How is Tori doing?" I ask.

Logan smiles. "She's been better. Just lost her job. But I

wouldn't call her Tori. She hates that nickname."

Tori never did have the career ambitions. She's probably back at her mother's house now, living the good life on the beach in California, until she finally decides she needs a little cash, like her brother, and gets a bartending job or something.

"Trust me, I don't plan on seeing her anytime soon, so you don't have to worry about me calling her Tori." I pick up my suitcase. "You working tonight, or do you have time to go grab a drink?"

Logan glances at his watch. "I'm already five minutes late to work. I should go, although I'd really rather be here."

"Don't worry; I'll be here for at least a couple of weeks. We will have plenty of time to grab a drink and hang out."

Logan grins as he walks backward toward the door, still looking at me. "I'm not worried about having time for us to hang out. I'm just disappointed that I'm going to miss the fight."

"Fight?"

Logan just continues to grin like the bastard that he is. "Have a good night. You might need to call a chiropractor for tomorrow. The couch is worse than the futon—or so I've been told."

Logan leaves me standing alone in the living room. I eye the couch; it looks ancient. A large indentation is on the cushion on one end; it's clear that Logan sits there every single time. The other end is scratched up from where his dog used to sleep. There is no way I'm sleeping on that couch. I don't know why I would anyway if there is a perfectly good bed just down the hallway.

I prepare myself for what is waiting for me down the hall. I know my friend too well. We always pulled pranks on each other as kids. So, I'm sure he did something stupid to the bed after I complained about my back last time. If the bed is unusable, I'll just buy a new one.

I carry my bag down the hallway, trying to think of what I

would do to him if I wanted to prank him. Pour beer in his bed. Put books under one corner of his bed, so it's crooked. Just remove the mattress completely.

I reach for the handle of the door just as it turns.

I frown.

The door swings open, and the last person I expected to see is standing in the doorway.

Tori.

Except this woman can't be Tori. Tori is an awkward high schooler with braces, frizzy hair, and oversized clothes that don't fit her body. The person standing before me is all woman. Her dark jeans make her legs look long as they hug over her curvy hips. Her gray V-neck accentuates her waist and cleavage, which shows just how much she has grown up since the last time I saw her. And her auburn hair shines as it frames her face, which is no longer covered in freckles and instead looks smooth and flawless.

Tori frowns when she sees me. "What are you doing here?"

I smirk. "I could ask you the same question."

"I'm here to see my brother." She places her hands on her hips, and her breasts automatically push up against her shirt.

My cock twitches at the sight.

I force my eyes to look into her deep brown eyes instead of at her breasts. I never thought that I would have that problem when it came to Tori. She's my best friend's little sister. We used to make her life miserable. I can't fuck her and then leave her. Logan would kill me.

"Same."

Her eyes darken as she glares at me and then down at the bag I'm carrying. "You'd better be taking that to a hotel."

"I'm not staying at a hotel. I'm staying here. That way, I can get plenty of time to see Logan and torture you, just like old times."

She narrows her eyes and steps forward, trying to intimidate me even though she is only half my size. "Then, you can sleep on the couch. And, as far as torturing me goes, that won't be happening. I'm not the scrawny teenage girl I was before."

I laugh as I look her up and down. "You might have filled out a little since the last time I saw you, but you still barely come up to my chest. I can torture you as much as I want, and you won't be able to do a thing about it."

Her nostrils flare, and her face turns bright red.

"I have an important meeting I need to get to in the morning. I really need to go to sleep. Give me the bedroom tonight, and maybe we can work something out tomorrow." I wink at her.

Her eyes deepen, and I think I see a vein popping out of her head. She's so angry with me.

"This is my room!"

"Who is the one who has to get up to go to work in the morning? From what I heard, it sure isn't you. You can nap in my bed while I'm at work."

"No. I'm not sleeping on the couch. You are."

I laugh. "Oh, come on, Tori. You're tiny. You can easily fit on the couch."

"My name is Victoria, not Tori."

I cock my head to the side and stare at her breasts. She's right, a cute nickname like Tori just doesn't cut it. "I can see that."

She frowns but doesn't cross her arms over her chest, like I expected. She doesn't hide and cover her body. She points her finger toward the living room. "Enjoy the couch. I've heard it will give you one wicked neck- and backache in the morning."

She turns and walks back into the bedroom. She grabs the door to slam it shut, but I grab it, stopping it just before it reaches the frame.

I push it back open and take a step forward so that I'm

standing in the doorway, and my face is inches from hers. I watch as her breathing picks up. I watch her lick her lips, like she is preparing for me to kiss her. I watch her eyes deepen at the thought of what my body could do to her.

Victoria wants me. Badly. I always thought that she secretly had a crush on me when we were kids. She used to try to hide it, but I knew. But, now, she isn't hiding it. Despite how much she hates me, she wants my body with the same passion.

Torturing her is going to be more fun than when we were kids.

"We could always share the bed." I wink again.

The spell she's under quickly breaks. "Out. Now."

"No."

"Out."

"No."

"Don't make me slam your hand in this door."

I laugh. "You couldn't if you wanted to."

She starts trying to push the door shut on my hand, but the door barely moves.

I raise an eyebrow, and she huffs but stops. In that second, I can see the adorable little girl she used to be.

I grin.

"Can't you be a gentleman for once in your life and let me sleep in the bed?"

"Really? You're going to play the *I'm a woman, so I deserve the bed* card."

"No, I'm playing the *I was here first; I have equally important things that I need to be up for in the morning; yes, I'm a woman, so I'm held to a different standard than you; and I don't want to have circles under my eyes from lack of sleep* card."

I pretend to consider what she is saying for a second. "Sorry, life ain't fair."

I step completely inside as she stumbles backward.

"Are you going to take your stuff and get out, or do we have to do this the hard way?" I ask.

"I'm not going anywhere."

I grin. "Hard way it is."

I scoop up her duffel bag and throw it over my shoulder, and then I turn my attention to Victoria. She's standing at the foot of the bed with her arms crossed over her chest. Her eyebrows are raised, like she doesn't believe I will actually force her out of this room. She's forgotten what I'm like if she thinks I'm not going to do anything.

"You wouldn't."

I walk over to her, bend down, and grab her ankles as I toss her over my shoulder.

Victoria screams and beats at my back as I carry her over my shoulder.

"Put me down! This is ridiculous!"

I don't put her down. I carry her down the hallway, loving how it feels to control her like this and have her so close to me. She smells like the ocean. I can smell the salt in her hair as I hold her.

I toss her down onto the couch and drop her duffel bag next to her.

"You're an asshole!"

I nod. "I'm an asshole who is about to get a very good night of sleep."

She huffs. "You haven't changed."

I shrug. "Why mess with perfection?"

She shakes her head as she sits on the couch. I turn to walk back to the bedroom, but I already know what she's going to do. She's not going to give up this easily. At least the Tori I used to know wouldn't.

I can hear her running after me, but I'm much faster than her. I always have been. I run into the bedroom before she even makes it to me. I stand in the doorway, marking my claim, as she stands in the hallway, breathing hard.

I smirk. "You'll never win, Tori. You might as well give up."

She sighs. "Fine. You win." She throws up her hands in the air and starts walking back to the living room.

I watch her ass sway back and forth and then shut the door, happy with my victory. I don't know why it's so fun to tease Victoria, but it is. I love making her miserable. But I do really need to get a good night's sleep so that I'm fresh for tomorrow.

I turn to grab my bag when I realize that I left it in the hallway. I open the door to get it and then freeze. My bag is no longer in the hallway.

I shake my head and smile just a little. I should have known that Victoria would pull something like this.

I walk down the hallway and find her standing in the only bathroom with the door open, her makeup and hair crap already spread all over the bathroom vanity, as she begins to tie her hair up into a ponytail.

"What did you do with my bag?"

"You lost your bag? That sucks."

I frown. "No, I didn't lose it. You took it."

She purses her lips and scrunches her face, like she's thinking real hard. "Nope. I don't remember any bag. Sorry."

She slams the bathroom door in my face before I have a chance to argue with her any further. I sigh. The apartment is tiny. Just two bedrooms, one bathroom, and an area that functions as the living room, kitchen, and dining room—combined. It can't be that hard to find where she hid my bag.

But, after searching for twenty minutes, I can't find it. And, now, I'm mad.

Victoria finally comes out of the bathroom. The makeup is gone from her face, her hair is up, and she is wearing flannel bottoms with a tank top and no bra. My eyes are glued to her hard nipples, which are pushing against the thin purple shirt.

She clears her throat, and I look up at her.

"Where is my bag, Tori? This is getting old."

She smiles. "Give up the bed, and I'll show you where your bag is."

I laugh. "That's not how this works. Tell me where my bag is."

She smirks and brushes past me. "Good night, Carter."

My bag has to be in the bathroom. I step inside and search for it, but I can't find it. I take a deep breath as I step back out. It's fine. Logan and I are close to the same size. I'll just borrow a suit from him for tomorrow, and then I'll find my bag after my meeting. I'm not going to let her get to me.

I find a spare toothbrush and brush my teeth, and then I head to bed. I remove my clothes and then climb into the queen-size bed. My body melts into the bed after a long day of traveling. She thinks she's won by taking my clothes, but I would take this soft bed any day over that damn couch. *Who cares that I don't have any clothes?*

Music starts blaring loudly down the hallway.

I groan. *Really? That's what she's going to try?*

She can't sleep, so she's going to try to keep me from sleeping as well. I laugh. The joke's on her because I can sleep through anything. It's a talent really.

I roll over and throw the covers over my head, knowing that I will be asleep in a few seconds—as soon as I can get Victoria out of my head. She's started a war that I can't wait to finish. She thinks I was cruel to her before. Well, she hasn't seen anything yet. Because, now, I know her real weakness.

Me.

She wants my body. She wants me to fuck her. And I know exactly how to torture her and win this war.

VICTORIA

I SMILE SWEETLY at Lily as I hold back a yawn. I might be completely exhausted after staying up all night, preparing for this meeting, but it was worth it. I'm killing this meeting.

When I first arrived at her doorstep, Lily wasn't sure that she should even continue to try to run for the Senate, but in the last hour that I've been here, I've seen her skepticism slowly turn into optimism. I'm going to get this job.

The only thing standing in my way is Carter.

I was shocked to see him standing in my doorway when I opened the door at Logan's. I'll have to remember to kill my brother later for not telling me that Carter would be staying with him as well. But I shouldn't have been that shocked. I know what Carter does for a living. I should have known he'd be all over Lily, trying to get this job. He didn't fool me with his *I'm here to see my best friend* speech. He's here to get this job.

He just doesn't have a clue that I'm here for the same reason.

That's why I moved my meeting up earlier. I knew I would need to get to Lily first to have a chance at competing with Carter. I know he has a lot more experience than I do, but that doesn't mean he is the best person for the job.

I just wish I could have been there this morning when he realized that I turned off his alarm and that his clothes were all covered in beer. I would have loved to see the expression on his face. He thinks he can win this fight, but he's wrong. I have years of pent-up frustration from all the times he and my brother teased me. Now, it's time for payback. And nothing is going to be sweeter than me landing this once-in-a-lifetime job instead of Carter.

Although it was incredibly fun to sneak into his room and turn off his alarm, carrying in his beer-soaked suitcase. My cheeks flush when I think about him lying naked from the waist up in bed. He was always good-looking, but now he's a buff man. A man who, from what I've heard, has dated his fair share of women. He's a man who most women would die to have. He has the body of an athlete, the money of a prince, and the wit of a jester. And, when I saw him lying naked in the bed, all I could think about was how badly I wanted to slip in next to him. Not how angry I was at him for taking that bed away from me.

"Victoria, are you okay?" Lily asks.

I clear my throat and drink a sip of water, trying to get my cheeks to stop flushing and my mind to move away from Carter.

"Sorry. So, what do you think of my ideas?"

Lily smiles, looking back at the plans I have laid out of how I think she can manage to still keep the public on her side and make a real run for the Senate.

"You certainly have given me a lot to think about. I thought I was done when..."

I nod. She can't even speak about what happened. I'm not sure I would be able to either if a sex tape of me with a man who wasn't my fiancé was exposed on national TV.

"I would love to work for you, Lily. I think, together, we would make a great team. I know you think that things look bleak right now, but I promise, come election time, no one will even remember this. I'll make sure of that."

Lily smiles sweetly at me and nods. I haven't convinced her. Not yet at least. I want to stay here all day, talking with her until she's persuaded. But I can't. I've made the best argument I can, and now, it's up to her to decide what she wants to do next.

"I would love to work with you, too, Victoria. From what you've presented here today, it's clear that you are one of the best, and I have no doubt that, with you by my side, we could conquer the world. I'm just not sure if my heart is in it anymore."

I nod. "I understand. But I don't think you should give up on your dreams because of one hiccup. You can do this, Lily. We can do this together."

I take Lily's hand and give it a squeeze. Through my years in this business, I've learned that the best way to connect with a client is to connect with them emotionally. I have to gain their trust, and the best way to do that is to treat them like a friend, not like a client. She needs to trust me completely if we are going to work together. She has to be able to tell me anything.

"Thank you for coming. I don't have too many friends in this world right now, and it's been nice to just talk to someone and to realize that my life isn't over."

"It definitely isn't."

We both stand, and I give her a quick hug.

"I'll call you tomorrow and see where your head is at. Unfortunately, this is something you need to decide on quickly, so we can start spinning the news in your favor before the public has totally made up their minds about you. But, even if you decide that this is not what you want, you can always count on me being here for you as a friend."

I pick up my oversized purse that functions as my briefcase, and I turn and walk out the door of her second-floor office where she works as a lawyer, which is situated in a larger building that contains several offices.

I haven't walked far when I bump into a hard chest. I should step back, giving the man some space, but I linger, keeping my face against his chest as I breathe in the manly scent of his after-shave. My body tingles as his hands go to my waist. He hesitates for a second as well, not sure if he wants to pull me closer or push me away. Finally, he gently pushes me away from him.

I look up, hoping to find a sexy stranger standing in front of me, who I can ask out for a drink, hopefully leading to dirty things later tonight. I could use the distraction and an actual bed to sleep in tonight. And, if his smell and firm grip on my body are any indication, I would love to get in his bed.

My heart immediately hardens to that idea when I realize who is standing in front of me.

Carter.

His eyes widen when he sees me. "What are you doing here? Trying to sabotage my meeting?"

I smile. "No, despite what you think, my life isn't all about you."

He smirks. "It should be."

I resist the urge to punch him in his chiseled, alluring face and wipe the smug expression off his face. But, man, does he look good with a cocky expression and a tailored dark gray suit. If he wasn't such an asshole, he would be exactly my type. Ambitious, confident, good-looking. The bad boy I shouldn't want because I know he will burn me in the end. That's exactly who he is, and even forgetting our history together, his bad boy reputation is the reason I shouldn't want him. If only I could figure out how to turn off the button inside me that finds him far too attractive for what is healthy for me.

The way Carter is looking at me isn't helping either. His eyes are searing into my body as he studies my black stilettos, my dark gray pencil skirt, and my purple blouse. He doesn't hide the fact that he is imagining what it would be like to remove each item of clothing from my body. He stares for far too long, lingering over what he finds sexiest—my legs and breasts.

I bite my lip, and his eyes immediately go to my lips.

Please suck on my lip, I think.

No, what am I thinking? He's the devil.

The devil who is amazing in bed—or so I heard from half of my high school.

"I think you have ketchup on your lip." His thumb brushes against my lip before I can stop him.

He stares at the red liquid on his thumb, smells it, and then tastes it. "Nope. It's blood from you biting your lip so hard to keep from kissing me."

I glare at him. "I don't want to kiss you."

He laughs. "You should tell your body that."

I roll my eyes. *I'm not going to let him goad me.*

He cocks his head to the side. "I never thought I'd see you in a dress. You look good, Tori."

"Victoria. And it's a business skirt, not a dress."

He nods. "I thought you hated dressing up."

"No, I hated dressing up because you always ruined whatever I was wearing. So, what was the point?"

He looks from me to Lily's office behind me. "So, you hoping that Lily can help you get a job?"

I smirk. "Something like that."

He studies my eyes for a second. "You can't seriously think that you can come in here and get the crisis PR job to fix all of her problems, do you? Lily's life is a mess right now; she needs an expert. Not someone who just got fired and has zero work experience."

"I was laid off, not fired. And I am an expert. Just because I don't have a flashy business card and my own business doesn't mean that I don't know what I'm doing. I've been doing this for almost as long as you. I know what Lily needs and how to solve her problems. We just had a great discussion. She and I will be working together."

Carter laughs. "Not after I talk to her."

I narrow my eyes. "Oh, that's right; I forgot. You plan on sleeping with her to get the job. Lily's better than that. It won't work."

"I don't need to sleep with anyone to get the job. I actually make a living from doing this. I have an entire company that relies on me. I have employees. What do you have?"

"I'm getting this job."

He steps closer to me until his face is inches in front of me. My breathing picks up. I don't know whether I want to slap him or kiss him. Maybe both.

He grins. "We'll see."

I grin, too, because I know, if Lily picks anyone, it's going to be me. I'm more prepared than Carter. I'm better than him. I laid out a superior plan. And I'm more trustworthy than Carter. It's not a fight between the two of us; it's a fight to convince Lily to continue to pursue her career.

"And, as far as fucking someone goes, it looks like you are the one in need of a good fuck," he says, glancing down at my nipples, which are hard because of him.

I roll my eyes. "It's cold in here."

"Sure it is."

I glance down at where his cock is straining against the zipper. "I could say the same about you."

"I'm always down for a good fuck, Victoria. Just name the time and place."

I shiver when he says my name. Partly because I'm so used to him calling me Tori and partly because I love how he says it. I really need to find the off button on my hormones, or he is going to have the upper hand and take advantage of my ridiculous body that I can't control.

He wants me, too. He acts like he is in charge, but I know that control will vanish as soon as I show up, naked, in his bed.

I hate him. I can't really fuck him. I can't give him the satisfaction of winning.

But I can make him pay for all the pain he has caused me. Carter doesn't seem like the type who falls in love easily. So, it would be next to impossible to make him fall in love with me, only to rip out his heart. But I can make him *lust* after me. I can drive him wild with my body while denying him the one thing he wants.

I can destroy his career.

I can wreck his friendships.

I can drive him mad as he waits for a fuck that will never happen.

The door behind me opens, and Carter's attention immediately goes from me to Lily. I watch Carter as he takes in Lily. While I'm all business, albeit in a sexy business dress, Lily exudes beauty without even trying. He forgets I'm even here as he stares only at her.

I thought he wanted me, but from how he is looking at Lily, it's clear now that it's not me he wants. It's her. It only makes me want to hurt him more. I want to get this job and destroy everything he's worked so hard to get.

4

____

CARTER

THE SECOND LILY APPEARS, I give her my complete attention. Partially because she needs to know that this is the type of attention I would give her if she became my client and also because, if I keep looking at Victoria, I'm going to throw her over my shoulder and go fuck her in the restroom. And, as much as I want to forget about my job and just fuck Victoria, I won't. My career always comes first. Always.

My dick will get plenty of action later. It just won't be touching Victoria. Logan would kill me, and she's not my type anyway. Lily's my type. I should focus on fucking Lily, but first, I need to land the job. It should be easy if Victoria is my only competition.

"Lily, it's great to see you again," I say, walking over to her and kissing her on the cheek.

She smiles sweetly, and her eyes light up. "It's great to see you, too. Although I wish it were under better circumstances."

I shrug. "I've seen worse. It's nothing I can't fix."

She laughs. "Trying to sell me before we even get into my office?"

"Is it working?" I ask with my most mischievous grin.

She shakes her head but says, "Maybe. Come on in."

I follow her inside, glancing back to get one last glimpse of Victoria. But she's already gone. I ignored her, and she vanished.

I take a seat at the table, next to Lily. The room is more of a meeting room than an office, although it seems like it functions as both to Lily.

"It really is good to see you, Lily. I know your personal and work life aren't going exactly as you planned, but I'm happy that I'm here. It's been far too long."

"I missed you, too, Carter. I thought about calling you dozens of times in college."

I laugh. "Good thing you didn't. You wouldn't have liked college me."

She laughs. "Too much of a bad boy?"

"Something like that."

Lily blushes.

"So, tell me what you want now, Lily? What future do you want for yourself?"

She looks down at her hands.

I grab her chin to get her to look at me. "There is no wrong answer, Lily. Do you still want to be a senator? Do you want to change the world or not?"

"I don't know."

I narrow my eyes, studying her. I wasn't expecting that. The Lily I used to know was fearless and would have said *yes* without hesitation. I sit back in my chair.

"Well, I can't help you until you figure out what you want. If you want the world, I can give it to you. But I need to know that is what you want."

"Victoria said the same thing."

I sit up in my seat. "Victoria hasn't been doing this nearly as long as I have. If you want this, I'm your guy. I'm the one who can make it happen. Victoria is a sweet girl with good intentions, but she doesn't have the experience for a job like this."

"Because I fucked up my chances. There is no coming back from this."

"No, because you are an amazing woman who deserves the best. And I'm the best."

Lily smiles weakly.

"So, what do you want, Lily?" I take her hands in mine, forcing her to look at me and stop turning away.

She has to stop running from her problems. Even if she doesn't want to be a senator anymore, she still needs me to help her rebuild her image. She needs to face her troubles head-on. But I can't help her if she doesn't know what she wants.

"Do I have to answer now?"

"Yes. I'm not letting you run away from this. You need to decide what you want. And then I can help you."

She swallows hard.

"What do you want, Lily?"

"I want to be the next senator from North Carolina."

I grin. "Good girl."

She smiles brightly, finally showing me the confident girl I used to know.

"Today's a Sunday; it's not the best day to get your team caught up on everything or to do any interviews, so I'll spend today getting a plan together. Then, I'll have my team get your team up to speed, and we will start working on this tomorrow."

"Thank you, Carter. I'm not sure what I would do without you."

I hug her. "You would be just fine. But I'm going to make this a lot easier for you." I kiss her cheek. "Get some rest. You have a busy day tomorrow. But don't worry; I'll take care of everything."

———

"So, I see that you won the bedroom argument last night," Logan says as I take a seat at the bar next to him.

"Yeah, I did. But your sister won the clothes fight. I had to take all my clothes to the dry cleaners today for them to attempt to get the beer out of them."

Logan laughs.

"It's not funny. Your sister is annoying as hell."

"And you aren't?"

"When is she leaving anyway?"

Logan takes a drink of his beer. "Not sure. Probably when whatever job she came here for is finished."

I grin and sip my own beer.

"What's so funny?" Logan asks.

"I got the job that she came here for. So, my guess is, she won't be staying much longer."

Logan raises an eyebrow. "Victoria didn't get the job?"

I shake my head.

Logan frowns as he stares intently at his beer.

I slap him on the back. "Relax. I'm sure she will find something back in California."

Logan shakes his head as he stares at me with wide eyes. "You don't know Victoria at all, do you?"

"Of course I do. She's the same girl we used to pick on all those years ago when we were young."

Logan laughs. "She's not the awkward tomboy you used to know. And she's not going to just let you push her around and not fight back anymore."

"Well, it doesn't matter. Lily made her decision, and she chose me, not Victoria. She can fight all she wants, but the decision has already been made."

"Maybe. I don't want to get in the middle of things between my sister and my best friend. But, if I were to bet, I wouldn't count out my sister."

"Whatever. Let's just celebrate my victory tonight and forget about Tori."

I lift my beer, and Logan clinks his against mine. I take a sip. Logan raises the glass to his lips and then grins, lowering it and looking at something behind me.

I don't have to turn around to know who's standing behind me.

"Hello, Tori," I say, using the nickname that apparently drives her crazy.

"Hey, Logan," Victoria says, ignoring me to walk over to Logan.

They hug, and then Victoria takes a seat next to Logan at the bar.

"What can I get you to drink?" the bartender asks her.

"I'll take a beer," Victoria says. "And they will each take another beer as well." She slaps the cash down on the bar to pay for all of our beers.

I narrow my eyes at her as she slides my beer over to me.

"What's this for?"

She eyes me. "We are celebrating."

She lifts her glass, as do Logan and I.

"Did you find a new job back in California?" I ask.

She smirks. "No, Lily gave me the job."

I chuckle.

"What's so funny?"

"That you think Lily offered you a job."

"Well, she did."

"You must be mistaken because she offered me the job before I even left her office this morning."

"Then, you must be the one who misunderstood because I just got off the phone with her. I start tomorrow morning, bright and early."

I shake my head. "I don't want to embarrass you, Tori, but

she offered me the job." I pull my phone out of my pocket. "But we can settle this once and for all."

I dial Lily's number and wait for her to pick up.

"Hey, Carter. What's up?" Lily asks.

"I just ran into Tori."

"Who?"

"Victoria. She says that you just offered her the job of handling your PR. I just need you to verbally tell her that it isn't happening and that I'm the guy who will be handling everything."

There is a moment of silence and then, "Actually...I just hired her."

"What?"

"I hired both of you. I loved both of your approaches, and this is a big enough project that I thought hiring two PR firms would be worth my investment. She can loop you into her ideas tomorrow. I'm sure you will work well together."

I stare at Victoria as she smiles slyly at me. I don't know what she did to convince Lily that she needs both of us, but whatever it is, I'll change Lily's mind tomorrow. Tonight, I need to work on Victoria.

"We will meet you at seven at your office. Get some sleep, Lily. We have a lot of work to do tomorrow."

I end the call and then glare at Victoria. "What did you do?" I ask.

She sips her beer. "I got the job, didn't I?"

"No, you didn't."

"Then, why are you so upset?"

"Because she hired both of us."

Victoria's eyes widen as she looks at Logan, like he is going to be able to do something about the situation. "What did you do?" she asks her brother.

"Nothing. I haven't talked to Lily since high school, same as you."

"Logan Grant, don't you dare lie to me. I know you enjoy watching me and Carter fight. Is this some kind of sick joke to force us to work together? What. Did. You. Do?" Victoria stands, towering over Logan, grabbing on to the neck of his shirt. She's a tiny woman who shouldn't be able to threaten a man like Logan with anything, but right now, the rage building inside her gives me no doubt that she would be able to take on Logan or any other man.

"Lily and I had lunch today," Logan says.

Victoria releases him. "I knew it. What did you tell her?"

"I told her I wasn't going to get in the middle of this. She asked me for advice on deciding who she should choose and what she should do, and I told her I couldn't help her. That either of you would be able to do the job. That it was up to her."

"Some friend you are," I say at the same time Victoria says, "Some brother you are."

We glare at each other for a second before turning our anger back on Logan.

"This isn't a game, Logan. I'm not some teenager you get to play with for your amusement. This is my career you are messing with."

Logan stands up and grabs Victoria's arms. "That's why I didn't say anything. I didn't do anything. Maybe I should have reminded Lily that you two didn't get along, but I never thought she would choose both of you. I promise. I would never do anything to hurt you. Not anymore."

Victoria takes a deep breath. "I know." She looks at me. "I guess we will be working together."

"Or you could quit," I say, taking a drink of my beer.

She takes a seat back on the barstool. "I'm not quitting. I don't care how miserable you try to make my life while we work together. I'm not quitting. This is my chance to start my own company. This is my big break, and I'm not letting you jeopardize that."

I shake my head and push down the fury building inside me. Lily needs my help, and Victoria is just going to get in the way.

"You're jeopardizing your career by staying."

"You can't scare me off, Carter. I'm a different person than I used to be. I'm done taking your crap."

"Yes, you are definitely done taking my crap. That's why I got the bed last night."

"And your clothes were drenched in beer."

"Nothing a little dry cleaning can't fix."

I gulp down the rest of my beer before walking over to her. "Thanks for the beer, Tori. I'll see you at seven sharp. Make sure to get lots of rest on that couch. I have a lot planned for tomorrow."

"You'd better look sharp because I plan on blowing Lily away with my ideas, and I doubt she will want to keep you around. You'll be out on the streets, looking for a new job, so you'd better look good for your job interview."

I smirk. "I think I like the old Tori better."

She turns and pushes her breasts out. My eyes immediately go to her cleavage. I want to bury my face in her chest and taste her smooth skin. I want to flick my tongue over her hardening nipple. I want to hear her scream my name when I push my dick inside her. I want—

"Your dick seems to like the new me."

"My dick is happy with any woman with breasts and a nice body. But it knows better than to get involved with trouble like you."

She rolls her eyes. "I don't doubt that. I think you should just fuck Lily and leave me to handle the crisis."

"Oh, don't worry, Tori; I can multitask just fine."

I brush a strand of her hair behind her ear and watch as her face fights between flushing with anger or blushing with lust. I might not get to fuck Victoria, but she sure is fun to play with in other more torturous ways. She'll break. She can't stand me. I give her eight hours of working with me tomorrow and trying to put up with my crap before she quits and leaves the job to me.

5

—————

VICTORIA

I needed a plan.

And that's exactly what I spent all night doing. Coming up with a plan to knock Lily's socks off to ensure that Carter will get sent home. While he was sleeping in the comfortable bed, I was working. All night long.

That's two nights in a row without any sleep. But it will be worth it to watch Carter's smug smile being kicked off his face.

I yawn for the millionth time this morning.

Thank God I was able to find the biggest coffee that Starbucks makes to keep me awake all day.

"Good morning, Lily," I say as brightly as I can as I enter her office.

"Morning, Victoria," Lily says.

She looks happy and beautiful in her red dress while I look like a hot mess. I'm wearing a business suit, my hair is up in a bun, and I barely had time to apply any makeup.

"I'm excited to see what you and Carter come up with. Two days ago, I thought my life was over, and then both of you came into my life and showed me that my career wasn't over. I just need to regenerate it."

55

"I'd be happy to get started on showing you some of my new plans while we wait for Carter," I say, trying not to add anything snarky at the end.

"We should probably wait. That way, you don't have to share your plans twice."

I sigh. So much for blowing her so out of the water with my ideas that she doesn't even remember that Carter is coming.

A knock rattles on the door before it is thrown open. Carter walks in, dressed in a dark blue suit. Lily's and my eyes both go to the hot man standing in the meeting room. A man who is equally handsome and awful at the same time.

He prances into the room, with a gleam in his eyes. He very clearly got plenty of sleep last night.

I grab my coffee, trying to ignore him, and stifle a yawn. As the coffee cup reaches my lips, Carter smacks me hard on the back.

"Good morning, Tori," he says as the coffee spills all over myself.

"Morning," I say through clenched teeth, trying not to scream from the pain all over my body.

"Oh goodness, did I do that?" Carter says sarcastically, looking at the coffee now dripping all over my face, arms, jacket, and pants.

"Yes, but it's not a problem. No need to cry over spilled coffee," I say, wiping off my face with the back of my jacket sleeve. I won't let him know that he is getting to me. I'll just pay back the favor later.

I stand up to take my jacket off and see what I should do with my pants.

"Here, let me help you," Carter says, grabbing my jacket.

Lily looks straight at me with a giant smile on her face. So, as much as I want to knee Carter in the balls for spilling scorching hot coffee all over me, I don't. I pretend to smile and let Carter remove my jacket.

My hands wrap around my bare arms as I feel the pain of the burn all over. I should have worn a long-sleeved blouse instead of one without any sleeves. Maybe it would have protected me better from the burns.

"Oh my God! Victoria, are you all right? Your face and arms are bright red," Lily says from across the table.

"I'm fine."

I feel Carter's hand touch my shoulder, and I jump. He moves his hand away for a second and then touches me softer, moving me to look at him. When he sees what I'm sure is my bright pink face and arms, he darts out of the room.

"Do you want me to get you a change of clothes or something?" Lily asks.

"No, I'm fine. Really. It's just a little spilled coffee."

Lily eyes my arms though, and I know it looks bad. But the pain is already subsiding, so it can't actually be that bad.

Carter returns with a bowl of water and a washcloth. He sets the bowl on the table. "Put your wrist in the water."

I roll my eyes. "I'm fine," I say again, hating the attention I'm getting.

He ignores me and grabs my wrist. He sticks my wrist and forearm into the cool water. The burn on my arm soothes immediately. I voluntarily stick my other arm in. When I look down I realize that my arm is redder than I expected.

"Look at me," Carter says.

I do.

His eyes narrow as he studies my face. He quickly puts the washcloth into the water, wrings it out, and then places it against my cheek. I wince and pull away from the cool water. He places his hand under my chin and gently turns it back toward him as he cautiously places the washcloth on my face.

I close my eyes at the initial sting and then open them as the cool cloth starts to calm my burn.

Carter intensely stares at me while he holds the washcloth to my face and then slowly pulls it away. I remove my hands from the water and shake them off.

"I'm sorry. I didn't mean to hurt you."

I shake my head. "I'm fine. No damage done."

He tucks a strand of hair behind my ear.

I swallow hard, trying to push any feelings that are creeping up, the more he takes care of me.

"I'm fine," I say for the millionth time, trying to convince myself more than him. "It barely hurt. My skin is just sensitive."

I turn away from him before he does anything else to make my heart flutter. It's just an act. He doesn't really care if he hurt me. He never has before.

"Here's some ointment to put on your burns, Victoria," Lily says, handing me a tube.

"Thank you. Let's get started with the meeting though," I say, taking it from her.

Lily and Carter both look at me, still concerned. Lily rubs her ear while she exchanges glances with Carter like she is secretly passing a message to him that I don't get to know.

I sigh. "I'm fine. I promise."

I glance down at my phone to check the time. "I was hoping to share with you my thoughts on the plans first, but I suspect that our savior himself is here."

Lily looks at me with wide eyes, and Carter just stares.

I get up and run out into the hall. I sigh with relief when I see him waiting for me.

"You came."

Phillip, Lily's ex-fiancé, nods. "You were very persistent that I get here. Are you okay?"

I bite my lip to keep from screaming. "Yes. Just a hot mess, as usual. Come on, let's go inside, and I can share the plans with everyone."

I grab his arm because I'm afraid he is going to run, and I lead him into the meeting room.

"Oh my God! Phillip, what are you doing here?" Lily says as she runs over and throws her arms around his neck.

To my surprise, Phillip hugs her back. I stand to the side, smiling, as I clasp my hands together and watch their reunion. I wasn't sure that my crazy plan was going to work, but seeing how happy they are to see each other reassures me.

A knot in my stomach forms when I look over at Carter, though, who is unfazed by the interaction. I thought he would be concerned that I just won Lily over. But he doesn't seem concerned; in fact, he seems amused.

"I came to help you. Victoria convinced me that you needed my help, so here I am," Phillip says.

Lily has tears in her eyes, which makes me tear up a little as I see them reunite. Phillip has no reason to forgive Lily or to help her in any way. They were engaged when she cheated on him. But, despite all the pain she caused him, he still loves her. I know it. And this proves it.

Phillip links his fingers with Lily's, and I about lose it. Such a simple gesture, but it's beautiful to observe the two of them together.

"I'm so sorry," Lily whispers.

As much as I want to stay and continue to grow envious as they reclaim their love for each other, I know I shouldn't. I motion with my head for Carter to follow me out and give them some privacy, and to my surprise, he does without protest.

I grin and sink into the couch in the lobby, down the hallway from Lily's office, as Carter leans against the wall.

"So, my plan is going even better than I thought."

He frowns as he walks over and sits next to me. "What is your plan exactly?"

"My plan is to give Lily and Phillip a chance to make up for real and then put them on every TV show, radio show, and newspaper, showing the love they have for each other. Lily won't hide her error, but she will make it clear that it was a mistake. Phillip will show forgiveness, and Lily will show her humility. They are a normal couple with real problems, just like everyone else."

"Your plan won't work."

"Are you crazy? Did you not see the two of them together? Their love is infectious."

"No, Phillip is too nice. He's not strong enough. He's a schoolteacher, not a powerful businessman. He's not seen as an equal to her. And, because of that, their love will never be seen as real. It will be clear that the only reason he's forgiven her is because she is way out of his league. Everyone will suspect that she is sleeping with hotter, more attractive men behind Phillip's back."

"You're wrong. You're just upset that Lily is going to love my plan, and you are going to be out of a job soon." I fold my arms across my chest and wince when I hit my burns a little too hard.

"Are you okay?"

I nod.

Carter takes my hand that has a burn on top of it. He lowers his lips and softly kisses the burn.

My eyes widen, and my breathing stops. It's just a stupid kiss on the hand, but it's one of the sweetest things a man has ever done for me. I don't understand how he could be so cruel one second and then so sweet the next.

He grins. "You don't trust me, do you?"

I shake my head.

"You shouldn't. Just like the people of North Carolina wouldn't trust Lily if she went back to her fiancé."

I frown. "You and Lily are different. You're an ass, and she's..."

He laughs. "She's a bitch."

I freeze when he calls Lily that. "I thought you liked her."

"Of course I like her. Lily and I are a lot alike, which is how I know your plan will never work."

He grins, and I know he has something up his sleeve. Something he isn't telling me.

I jump as a loud thump happens down the hallway.

"What was that?" I ask.

Carter frowns as he looks toward Lily's office. He starts jogging down the hallway, and I follow, not having a clue as to what is going on.

"Oh my God," I say and cover my mouth with my hands when I see two men fighting, covered in blood.

Lily is screaming for them to stop, and Carter is trying to figure out how to break them up without getting hurt himself.

Finally, Carter grabs hold of Phillip and pulls him away from the other man.

"What is going on?" I ask, looking from Phillip to the other man before it becomes clear who the other man is. I recognize the other man from the sex tape with Lily.

"What are you doing here?" Lily asks Jacob.

"I'm here for you. Your PR team asked me to come, so here I am. I'll do whatever you want to make this easier on you," Jacob says.

I turn to Carter, who is still holding Phillip back, realizing what he did. I brought Phillip, and he brought Jacob. We couldn't have fucked this up more if we had tried.

"Get the fuck out of here, you asshole! Lily is my fiancée!" Phillip shouts.

Jacob laughs. "I think that ended the second she got into my bed and agreed to be filmed."

Phillip tries to break free of Carter's arms, but he holds him back.

"Tell him to leave, Lily!" Phillip shouts.

But Lily can't say anything right now. Her tears are flowing down her cheeks, but otherwise, she's frozen. She has no idea how to handle this. This is the exact situation that Carter and I were hired to avoid.

"Escort Phillip out, Carter," I say.

Carter begins walking Phillip out of the building while I grab onto Jacob's arm and guide him out the back exit. I can hear Phillip fighting with Carter behind me, but to my surprise, Jacob doesn't fight me.

When I get him all the way outside, I ask, "What are you really doing here? You don't want to be involved in this, do you?"

Jacob shrugs. "Carter made me an offer I couldn't refuse."

"Money?"

"Something like that."

"Leave Lily alone."

"You don't have to worry about me. I get paid either way."

I frown and sulk back inside. That was a disaster. I walk back into the meeting room, just behind Carter.

"I'm so sorry, Lily. Victoria and I should have talked before we took action, and—"

"Shut your mouth," Lily says firmly.

I freeze, and so does Carter, who is sitting at the table in front of me.

"You two fucked up! Now, there is no way Phillip will take me back, and Jacob is too worked up to do anything you ask. I'm going to go get a massage and have lunch with a friend to try to get over my heartbreak at what just happened. You two have until I get back to come up with a plan together to fix this, or you're both fired." Lily walks calmly out of the room, leaving Carter and me alone.

I take a deep breath. *This is not my fault*, I repeat to myself over and over again. *This is Carter's fault.*

My eyes dart to him sitting calmly at the table. It doesn't matter whose fault it is. I'm going to be out of a job if I don't fix this.

I walk over and sit down on the opposite side of the table. I need to keep Carter at a distance if I'm going to have any control over the situation.

"You're mad," Carter says.

"Yeah, I'm mad. What were you thinking?"

He smirks. "I was thinking that I had years of experience in fixing people's problems, and I made a good living from doing it, so I should be the one who made the decisions."

I raise an eyebrow. "And you think that I don't have experience?"

"I know you don't have experience."

"I've been working in this industry, same as you."

"And what do you have to show for it? You lost your job; you didn't get promoted."

I frown. I hate him. I should just quit. But I won't give him the satisfaction of winning.

"Let's just figure out a solution to the mess you created."

He holds up a finger and then walks out without saying anything to me. It's annoying that he doesn't tell me what he is doing. But it gives me a chance to compose myself and calm down. We won't be any good to Lily if we spend the whole time arguing. I have to find a way to push through my feelings and be civil with him. No more fighting.

Carter walks back in a few minutes later, carrying a large coffee cup in his hand. I glare at him for getting himself a coffee after he spilled mine all over me.

I realize what I'm doing and close my eyes. *He's just goading you. Don't let him do it.*

I open my eyes, and he isn't standing across the table from me. He's leaning over me as he places the coffee cup in front of me.

"A peace offering," he says before sitting in the seat next to me.

I smile. "Let's get to work."

He holds my gaze for far too long before he says, "Where do you want to start?"

I don't know why he's being so nice to me. It's either from guilt from spilling coffee on me or ruining my plans for Lily, but whatever the reason, I'm not going to waste the moment.

6

CARTER

I FUCKED UP.

Not by convincing Jacob to come here today. I know that my instincts were correct. That Jacob would have been the best way to get the public back on Lily's side.

I fucked up by letting myself feel anything toward Victoria. I don't have feelings. Ever. I'm ruthless and uncaring. It's why I'm so good at my job. I never care about my clients. I just do what's best for them even if they hate me at the time. They always thank me afterward.

And, now that I've let myself care about Victoria, I don't know how to shut it off. I don't even feel anything that loving. I just feel guilt and concern. I've hurt Victoria countless times. But today was the first time that I didn't like it. I didn't like seeing her in physical pain. I didn't like the emotions it evoked in either of us.

"Carter, are you listening to me?"

I blink, trying to come back to the real world instead of the world of torture I have created for myself in my head. A world where I want Victoria, but I can't have her.

"To every word."

She frowns. "Then, what was I saying?"

"You said, 'Carter, are you listening to me?'"

She can't stifle the tiniest of grins from her lips. It makes me happy to see her smile.

"Before that."

"That you feel the best way to move forward is to show Lily as a strong, independent woman who doesn't need a man by her side. Don't paint the men as monsters but not as saints either. Just do one interview with another strong, independent woman who will want to address the sex tape but then will focus on the issues that Lily wants to tackle as a senator instead of doing dozens of interviews, like the plan was before."

She clears her throat. "You were listening."

"I have an impeccable memory. Anything I hear or see, I will remember."

She sips her coffee to keep from yawning. I know she stayed up all night, preparing for this. She's smarter than I gave her credit for. Most of her ideas are spot-on, and she has a backup in mind for every scenario. If we didn't hate each other so much, I would offer her a job. But her exhaustion is going to lead to mistakes. She might think she has the same level of experience as me, but having to spend all night formulating a plan shows me just how little experience she actually has. She's talented, but she needs someone to harness that talent.

"What do you think?"

I lean forward in my chair until I'm close enough to smell the coffee mixed with her perfume. "I don't think you care what I think."

She leans forward in her chair as well. "What do you think?"

"I think your ideas are good."

"Just good?"

I grin. "Better than good. But you have some flaws that you still need to work out."

"Yeah? And what are those?"

"You haven't slept in two days, so you aren't thinking clearly."

"What are the flaws in my plan?"

"You'll figure them out after a good night's rest."

She rolls her eyes. "Tell me now. We already screwed up once with Lily. We can't do that again. We are supposed to be working together to ensure that we don't mess this up anymore. That means, there can't be any secrets. We have to tell each other everything."

I lean back in my chair as I rub the back of my neck. She watches me.

"I'll make sure that we don't fuck up again. My reputation is on the line, too. But I want to help you grow. And you will never grow if I just tell you what you fucked up. I'll guide you, but you have to figure it out for yourself."

"Why are you trying to help me?"

I get up out of my chair and walk over to get my laptop. Then, I plug the projector into it. I'm trying to help her because I don't know how to turn my emotions off now that I've turned them on. I don't know why, but I actually enjoy listening to her voice. She talks so confidently about what she wants. It's nice, hearing her. It's nice, being near her.

"It's because you feel guilty for spilling coffee on me, isn't it?"

"No, it's because, when I see someone with talent, I can't help but nourish that talent."

"Was that a compliment?"

Victoria bites her lip, and I ache to have that lip in my mouth. I don't know what's come over me, but right now, my brain is obsessed with her.

Lily chooses that moment to walk back into the room. I knew she was coming back soon. She's been gone for hours, and I have an instinct when it comes to clients. This isn't the first time a client has walked out on me.

"Do you have a plan, or am I firing you both?" Lily asks. She folds her arms across her chest, and her face is stiff and rigid. Gone are the tears from earlier. Gone is the anger. She's all business now.

I can feel the nerves oozing off of Victoria as she sits at the table. She has a thorough plan, but I know it makes her nervous not to have visuals and a written plan for Lily. She wants to look as professional as she can. She thought she would have more time.

I click on the projector, and my plan pops up on the screen. I should be nice and let Victoria talk about the plan while I show the visuals. Our plans are similar enough that it doesn't really matter anyway. But I'm not nice. And the longer I pretend to be nice to Victoria, the more likely it is that she is going to get hurt later on. I'm the kind of person who would fuck her and leave her without a second glance.

Victoria doesn't deserve that. She doesn't deserve that kind of pain. Being an ass to her now is the only way to keep me from breaking her heart later on. She needs to hate me. So, I'll make her detest me by presenting our ideas as my own, by myself. And then she'll hate me.

———

My plan works. Victoria hates me.

I can feel it from the second she walks into Logan's apartment.

"Where is he?" I hear her ask Logan in the living room from where I'm sitting on the bed with my laptop on my lap.

She's angry, and she should be. I don't hear Logan's answer, but I'm sure that he's pointed her in my direction because I can hear her stomping down the hallway toward me.

"What the hell was that?" she yells, throwing my bedroom door open.

"I did my job. You can't hate me for that."

"No, you weren't doing your job. You stole my ideas and claimed them as your own."

I fold my arms across my chest, amused at how worked up she gets. I think that's why I like teasing her so much. She's adorable like this.

"I didn't steal your ideas."

"Yes, you did! I told you every single idea, and then you shared them with Lily. Now, she thinks they were all your ideas."

"I didn't steal your ideas," I say again.

The look she gives me is beyond anger. Her nostrils are flared, and her face is red, but her eyes suddenly stop on my bare chest.

"Are you naked?" she asks, changing the subject.

"Does it matter if I am?"

Her eyes drop to the sheets covering me from the waist down. "Yes. You shouldn't be naked."

"Why? Because you won't be able to control yourself if I am?" I smirk.

"No...because, um...because I want to have a serious conversation with you, and I can't do that if you're trying to distract me with your body."

I grab the top of the sheets and slowly push them down. Her eyes stay glued to them as I reveal my boxers beneath them.

"Put some clothes on."

"I have clothes on. This is my room. You entered without knocking. I can wear whatever I want."

She huffs. "Why did you steal my ideas?"

"I. Didn't. Steal. Your. Ideas."

She glares at me.

"If you recall, I had all the same ideas already written down on my laptop before you started blabbing them to me. I came up with those ideas yesterday and wrote them down as a backup plan because I figured you would somehow mess up my original plan."

She places her hands on her curvy hips while pushing her breasts out at the same time. "You messed up my plan."

I nod and smirk, which only angers her more and makes my cock desperate to fuck her. I love her pouty mouth. I love how she stands confidently in my bedroom, still in her coffee-covered outfit instead of changing. I love how she hates me.

"So, what did you talk to Lily about after I left?" I ask.

"Wouldn't you like to know?"

I raise an eyebrow. "I thought we were a team, that we needed to share everything with each other, so we don't fuck up Lily's life again."

She casually runs her hand across the footboard of the bed. "I realized my first flaw."

"Oh, and what is that?"

"That I thought we could ever be a team. You don't have a heart. Whatever niceness you showed toward me was all an act."

I nod. "You're learning."

She flicks her shoes off into the corner of the room.

"Now, get out of my bed," she says.

I laugh. "This isn't your bed; it's mine."

"No, tonight, it's mine. And don't even think about throwing me over your shoulder again and carrying me out. You wouldn't dare do that, not with Logan here."

She's right. I wouldn't. Logan would kick my ass if he saw me doing anything to hurt her. But he also wouldn't get in the middle of this.

"I'm not going anywhere."

"Fine. Be a stubborn ass."

She walks to the door and throws it shut. I cock my head, confused at what she is doing.

She turns and begins undoing the buttons on her blouse, swiftly moving down until all the buttons are undone.

"What are you doing?"

She throws her shirt off onto the floor. "I'm going to bed."

She quickly undoes the button and zipper on her pants and pushes them down.

I know I'm sitting here, gaping at her hot body, giving her exactly what she wants, but I don't care. I can't help myself. No man could stop from getting turned on by watching her. I'm shocked that she doesn't have a boyfriend or fiancé or husband.

She walks over to my side of the bed. She puts her finger under my chin and lifts it up, closing my jaw.

"It's not polite to stare, you know."

She tries to move away, but I grab her wrist.

"It's not polite to tease."

"Who said I was teasing?"

I narrow my eyes at her.

She reaches behind her with her free hand and undoes her black lace bra. She slides one arm out of it, and I immediately release her other hand to watch her bra fall to the floor.

I watch her bite her lip out of the corner of my eye, but I can't take my eyes off her breasts. Her nipples are hard, begging for me to take them into my mouth. I grip my hands to keep from feeling the fullness and softness of her breasts.

She clears her throat, and I look up at her. She thinks she's won this fight. That, if I show her how badly I want to fuck her, she will have the upper hand. So, I do the only thing I can to keep my power.

I pull her onto the bed. I toss her over me onto the bed next to me, and I climb on top of her, pinning her to the bed beneath me. Our faces are millimeters apart as we both breathe fast. She licks her bottom lip, anticipating a kiss that I'm desperate to give her.

In all our years together, growing up, I never thought to taste her lips. I never thought to date her. To make out with her. To get her naked. Fuck her. But then the girl I used to know would never have dared to get naked in front of me just so she could win a fight.

I move just a little closer, taking every second of this in because this is the closest I will ever get to her. I won't fuck her. Even if I wanted to, she hates me too much to let me touch her. This is just a game to her.

"Good night, Tori." I roll off of her, rolling away from her to turn off the light.

She growls lightly in her throat.

"Disappointed, Tori?"

"No, just shocked that you are able to resist me."

I roll back over and throw my arms around her, pressing my dick against her ass. "You want me to be nice and caring and do what's right, right?"

She nods.

"This is me doing that."

I pull her tighter to me, showing her just how badly I want her. My cock pushes harder against her. And, if she listens closely, she will be able to hear my heart beating as fast as hers.

"Comfortable?" I ask, knowing that she won't say no. She's too stubborn, just like me.

"Perfect."

I grin.

"Good night, Victoria."

She sucks in a breath, and despite how exhausted she is, I know she isn't going to be able to sleep a wink. I wish I had the same problem. I would love to remember every second of holding her tonight. I want to remember every curve, every smell, every sound. I want to hear her restlessness at the fact that I'm so close to her. I want to hear her gasp when my hand accidentally brushes against her breast. I want to know when she regrets ever undressing in front of me.

But I can't. I won't be able to stay awake. I know my body too well. I know that the second it realizes it doesn't get to fuck her, I'll be out, and I'll miss all the moments I'm desperate to remember.

7

VICTORIA

Damn it.

How stupid could I be to think I could win a fight with Carter Woods?

He's had years of practice in winning fights while I've just barely started learning how to fight back. And, now, I'm more exhausted than ever before. I'm not sure I slept more than an hour or two all night. Either his arms or his legs were wrapped tightly around me, even when he was fast asleep. His cock pushed hard against me, driving me mad. I've fucked plenty of men, but I've rarely slept all night in the bed with them. I'm used to sleeping on my own, and Carter made it impossible for me to sleep.

I didn't think he would have the strength to resist me, not when I was naked in his bed. I'm not sure if I would have actually let him fuck me or just taunted him to prove my point.

But it doesn't matter now. He's proven yet again that he can win any game. I just have to learn to win when he doesn't realize we are playing the game.

"Sleep well, Victoria?" he asks, stretching after getting a full night's sleep, releasing me for the first time all night.

I don't know whether to hate or love that his arms are no longer wrapped around me.

I give him a dirty look because I know he will know if I'm lying to him.

He smirks as his eyes drop down to my breasts. There's a gleam there I've found in his usual stare when he looks at me.

I don't cover my body. I let him see what he missed. I gave him plenty of chances to apologize. To have sex with me. Now, he needs to know how much of a mistake not fucking me was.

"I'm going to shower," I say, walking to the door so that he can stare at my ass.

"Don't use all the hot water!" he shouts when I open the door and walk out.

I sigh. I don't know what it's going to take to break him. I threw myself at him, naked, and he still didn't take the bait. He's winning, and I'm not sure how to stop him.

"Please put some clothes on, sis," Logan says as he walks down the hallway, shielding his eyes.

I grab a towel from the bathroom and cover up. "Sorry, I forgot you were here."

His eyes look at me and then the door to the guest bedroom that I left open. "Wait," he says, looking back and forth again. "You and Carter?" He looks to the bedroom door. "I'm going to kill him."

Logan starts storming down the hallway to give Carter a piece of his mind.

I bite my lip. I should say something. Let him know that Carter didn't fuck me. He just slept with me naked in his bed while he tortured me with his unrelenting touch and hotness. I might not be able to win against Carter, but at least Logan can chew him out.

———

I step into the office with a fake smile on my face when I realize that Carter is already here. I don't know how he got here so fast since I occupied the only bathroom until the last possible second before I needed to leave to get here on time. But, somehow, he looks clean and completely put together, as he always does.

"Good morning, Lily," I say, ignoring Carter.

He stares me down as I enter.

"Good morning," Lily says, seeming relaxed, which is good since she has the television interview this evening.

Her phone buzzes, and she answers.

I turn my attention to Carter. "You look surprisingly clean and well dressed for someone who didn't have access to a bathroom this morning."

He leans back in his chair while I take a seat next to him.

"I used Logan's neighbor's bathroom. Katherine didn't mind me using her place in exchange for getting my company."

I raise an eyebrow. "So, you offered to sleep with her in exchange for using a bathroom? How desperate are you?"

He leans close to me. "Not as desperate as you are to have sex with me."

I push him away from me. He falls back in his chair with a thump, but it's not enough. I want to slap him in the face. I shouldn't feel that way. He's not mine. If he wants to sleep with the hot neighbor, he can. But I'm tired of him taunting me about it.

"Did Logan let you have it?" I ask, knowing that will at least push his buttons a little.

"Logan doesn't know what he's talking about," Carter says, staring off into space.

I sigh. "I should have told him that you didn't fuck me last night. But it was too fun for me to let him yell at you first."

"He knows I didn't fuck you," Carter says with a seriousness in his voice I wasn't expecting, turning back to me.

I tuck a strand of my hair behind my ear. "Then, what was all the yelling about?"

Carter swallows. "He thinks I'm going to hurt you."

I laugh. "You already have—about a million times. Nothing you do now can really hurt me." I sigh, running my hand through my hair, pulling out the few curls that I have. "Don't worry. I'll talk to Logan when I get back. You'll still be best friends."

"I'm not worried about my relationship with Logan."

My heart stops when I see how Carter is looking at me. I'm not sure what to think. I see the lust that was there last night, but I also see something else that I don't understand. There's a kindness that I haven't seen before, especially when he's looking at me.

"Sorry about that," Lily says, hanging up the phone.

I swallow and turn to give my full attention to Lily. If I'm going to beat Carter, then I have to focus everything I have on this job.

"So, prepare me for this interview," Lily says with a large smile on her face that looks as fake as my warm feelings toward Carter.

"I have a list of questions that they will most likely ask you. How about we start with me just reading through them and you answering honestly? Then, we will go from there."

Lily twists her bracelet around her wrist as she swallows. "Sure."

She's nervous. Everything in her body is screaming just how terrified she is about this interview. I never thought that Lily would be terrified of an interview. She loves the camera. But I guess, after what happened the last time she did an interview, I don't blame her. But it's going to take all day to get her feeling comfortable again.

I eye Carter out of the corner of my eye. I'm ready for him to argue with me, saying that my plan isn't the best way to start our preparations. But he doesn't say anything. Maybe he will actually behave today.

I pull out my notes with the questions that I wrote up. "Let's start with some easy questions. Why do you want to be a senator?"

"Because I want to make a difference. I'm tired of always being the pretty girl who is just meant to marry the attractive guy, and that's it. I want my life to be more than just some hot body that men ogle. My passion is helping children. I want to make sure that no child ever has to go a day hungry. I want to make sure that all children have access to the best education. I want to make sure that all children can get the medical care they need. And I want to be a role model to little girls everywhere, showing that they can grow up and become a powerful woman who can bring about change in the world."

I smile. Her answer isn't perfect, but it doesn't need to be. The way she spoke with such sincerity—that's what is important here.

"Don't mention yourself as a role model to girls. It's going to trigger too many questions about how you could be a role model for girls when you made a sex tape. You also need to dig deeper," Carter says.

I glare at him. He's going to make her lose what little confidence she has on the first question. She's going to be a mess by the end of our session if he keeps nitpicking her like this.

"Actually, I think you were amazing, Lily. I wouldn't change anything. Let's just go through all the questions, and then we can discuss how to make the most important answers better," I say.

Lily's eyes dart back and forth between the two of us.

Carter turns to me with his own devilish glare, his face tense, and I can tell he is doing everything he can to hold back his anger. "I know you don't have a ton of experience in preparing people for interviews, but if we let her practice wrong, that is what she is going to remember when she gets asked questions in the actual interview."

He turns to Lily. "I'm not going to coddle you, like Tori wants to. You're better than that."

I can't hold back my anger and frustration with him. I thought we could be civil, for Lily's sake, but I guess I was wrong.

"Next question. What is the status of your relationship with your fiancé?"

Lily freezes as the tension rises. She's unsure of who to answer or what to say. We are making this worse. If she can survive the day with the two of us arguing, she will be able to survive any stupid interview questions thrown her way. I'm just not sure if I can put up with Carter for an entire day without killing him.

———

"I can't handle this anymore!" Lily screams, grabbing her head.

Carter and I both freeze, staring at her. We've spent the better half of the morning arguing about how she should answer each question. Every single question came with an argument. Every. Single. One.

I'm not surprised to see Lily breaking like this. She deserves better than what we are giving her.

"This was a mistake," she says, standing up and pacing back and forth in front of the table in the room we have been cooped up in.

I stand up and walk over to her. "I'm sorry, Lily. We will take it down a notch. You're doing great. If you can put up with us drilling you now, then you will do a great job tonight at your interview."

Her eyes widen, and I see the true fear and anger come out in one look.

"No." She strides over to her chair, grabbing her jacket and her purse.

Carter stands up, blocking her way to the door. He grabs on to her shoulders. "Relax, Lily. You got this."

She laughs. "I'm not worried about myself. I've done interviews countless times. I know what to say and what not to say. I know how to say charming things to distract the audience from what they should be worrying about. How do you think I got this far? But what I can't put up with is you two bickering. I thought I was being smart when I hired both of you, but now, I realize just how much of a mistake that was."

She takes a deep breath and then looks back to me. "I'm going to the salon to get my hair colored and get my nails done. Give me the interview questions."

I slowly walk over, handing her my notebook of questions.

She snatches them out of my hand. "I'll prepare for the interview on my own. And, when I get back, you two had better have worked out whatever shit is going on between the two of you. And, if I hear one more stupid argument, then I'm going to fire you both. I don't need this stress right now." She looks at Carter, who is still blocking her path to the exit. "Now, move."

He opens his mouth to say something but thinks better of it and steps out of her way. She stomps out of the room, leaving Carter and me alone in the meeting room.

"Great job," Carter says, snarky.

"You're an ass," I say, gathering my things.

I take Lily's lead and walk out. I know it is going to do nothing to solve our current predicament, but I can't let myself stay trapped in the same room with him for another second.

I march quickly out of the building, not caring that, by doing so, I'm probably losing yet another job and my best shot at starting my own firm. My head is already spinning with how I can salvage this, but my ideas all start with me strangling Carter to death because he is the root of all my problems. Every problem I've ever had started with him.

"Tori, wait," I hear Carter yell behind me as I continue down the sidewalk to my rental car.

I freeze. *Don't engage him. Just walk away. Give up. Let him deal with Lily. I can find a new job. I don't need this one client in order to start my career. That's what I should do. Just get in my rental, go back to Logan's, pack up my things, and get on the first flight back to California.*

But I can't give up so easily. I'm too stubborn for that.

I turn around. "What did you just call me?"

He cocks his arrogant head to the side. "You aren't running away, are you, Tori?"

I can't control myself anymore. I stomp over to where Carter is standing on the sidewalk, and I slap him. Hard. Across the face.

It's not one of my better moments as far as judgment goes, but I can't let him just get away with being the biggest jerk on the planet anymore. I'm tired of him hurting me even though I should be used to it by now.

He doesn't seem shocked that I hit him. In fact, he seems like that is exactly what he wanted. "I thought I couldn't hurt you anymore."

My nostrils flare, and my face turns bright red as I try to keep my breathing even and cold. "I lied."

He nods, putting his hands into his pockets, as he walks closer to me. "I know."

I take a step back. I don't want him anywhere near me.

"I'm sorry."

I pause at his words before walking backward, and he takes another step forward, gaining on me.

"You aren't capable of being sorry. At least, not toward me."

He nods. "You're right. I probably don't deserve your forgiveness, but does it make you feel any better to know that the past two hours have just been me goading you, trying to get you to break, so that I could prove to you that I'm still capable of hurting you?"

"No, it doesn't make me feel any better that you purposefully hurt me to prove a point."

He bites his lip, and I find myself staring far too intently at his damn lips. *How can I find a man I hate so sexy?* It shouldn't be possible.

He takes another step toward me until he's only a foot away from me. "I needed to know."

"Why?" I throw my hands up. "Why did you need to know that you could still hurt me?"

He reaches his hand out and lightly touches me on my bottom lip. "Because, believe it or not, I care about you."

I laugh. "You can't care about me. It's not possible."

His hand goes to the back of my neck before I realize what he is doing. He pulls me hard toward him. Our lips crash together in a hungry kiss. My eyes close the second our lips touch. My hands wrap around his neck, and my body responds to his. The kiss makes me forget about all the pain he's caused me. It makes me want him. It makes me ache for him. He takes complete control over my body with just one single kiss.

"No," I say, pushing him away from me. "I won't let you control me. You don't get to just kiss me and make everything better."

"How am I controlling you if this is what you want?"

"You think I want this?" I motion between us.

"I know you do. You can't kiss me like that and not want this."

I laugh. "I can. You can kiss me a million times, and I will never want anything more. There is nothing you can do to make up for the past. Nothing."

He narrows his eyes. "Even this?"

He scoops me back into his arms and kisses me again. My breathing stops as he kisses me. His tongue pushes deep into my mouth, begging me to let go of our past. To let him in.

I shouldn't. I know that, if I do, nothing but pain will follow. But, with his hand tangled in my hair, my body in his arms, his lips kissing me like I've wanted him to since the second I saw him again, I forget about the pain.

He gently pulls away, looking deep into my eyes, now asking for permission for a kiss that he just took from me again.

I slap him across the face again, but he doesn't let go of me. He just holds me tighter.

"I'm not yours. You don't get to control me. No one controls me."

I push his arms off of me, and I start walking down the sidewalk again although not as fast as before. I need to get out of here before I agree to do something stupid that would only leave me more broken than ever before.

He runs after me until he catches up with me. I expect him to grab my arm again and force me to stop, but he doesn't. He just walks next to me. Maybe he's tired of getting slapped.

"I'm sorry."

"Sorry isn't good enough."

"Why not? I know you want this as much as I do. I'm not saying that you should marry me. Just give me a clean slate to start over. Let me take you on a date. Let me fuck you. Give me a chance."

"You want to date me? Seriously?"

"Maybe."

I shake my head. "Why would I let go of everything that you have done to me when you give me no confidence that this is even what you want?"

"Because we can't keep doing this. Whatever is going on between us, it has to stop. We are destroying Lily and hurting our careers, all so that we can deny this sexual tension. If nothing else, at least maybe we should just fuck whatever this is out of our systems, and then we can move on and finally do our jobs."

"Fucking you won't get the time you cut my pigtails in kindergarten out of my system," I say, stopping as I glare at him. "Fucking you won't get the time you convinced my brother that girls were gross and wouldn't let him talk to me for a year even though I needed him." I take a step toward him as I let my anger through.

He doesn't take a step back even though I'm more than likely going to slap him again.

"Fucking you won't take away the time you shoved me off the playground and broke my arm."

He stands frozen, taking it all. Every horrible thing he has ever done to me hits him.

"Fucking you won't take away the time you said you would drive me home when it was freezing cold outside, and instead, slept with some girl while I had to walk home in a snowstorm without a coat."

I let all the horrible things he's ever done to me out. Every single one. Except one. I keep the worst for myself. If I told him, he would realize how much I cared about him when we were teenagers. If I tell him the worst thing that he's ever done to me, then he might try to ask for forgiveness. I might let go of the pain and actually forgive him. And I can't do that. He doesn't deserve my forgiveness.

"Are you finished?"

I cross my arms over my chest. "Why? You want to do something else to hurt me?"

"No, I want to tell you how truly sorry I am. I was fucked up as a kid. I had my own problems to deal with, but rather than deal with them, I took them out on you. Can you forgive me for what I did as a kid?"

"Yes, but I can't forgive you for what you've done as a man."

He swallows and looks like I slapped him even though I didn't.

"You're right. You shouldn't forgive me for hurting you now."

I nod, hating how silky and deep his voice sounds when he speaks. Because, if I listen to his voice too long, I will do anything he says.

I look into his damn eyes before I realize that it's a trap. His eyes are full of sincerity and lust. A deadly combination.

"What do you want, Victoria?"

And then he has to say my real name.

"Do you want me to let you have this job? Do you want me to go away and never see you again? Do you want me down on my knees, begging you for forgiveness for the rest of my life? What do you want?"

I bite my lip. I don't know what I expected to happen, but I never expected this. I could ask him to let me have Lily as a client. It would make my career if I did. But I won't. Unlike him, I want to win the job fair and square. I don't want to know that my whole career was made because Carter let me have it.

"Kiss me," I say.

His eyes search mine for just a second, as he's not sure if he actually heard the words that fell from my lips.

"Fuck it out of me. Fuck away all the pain. All the sexual tension. Fuck it all away."

8

CARTER

Victoria just told me to fuck her.

It's what I've been wanting to hear since the moment I saw her again. But, somehow, it feels like both the biggest mistake I could ever make and the best thing that I could ever do.

I gave her a chance to choose her career over me, and she chose me. She's putting her trust in me. A man who has hurt her more than any other person on this planet. I could use this to finish her for good or make her mine forever.

Or I could just fuck her. No emotions. No promises of anything more. Give her the best sex of her life. That's how I want her to remember me when this is all over. The best damn sex of her life. That's what I can give her.

I grab her face as I press my lips against hers. Her lips are the softest lips I've ever felt. When her tongue tangles with mine and her body presses against me, I know I just made the best damn decision of my life.

She's beautiful. But then she's always been beautiful. She's more than that now. She's hot. Her body fit and curvy. She's smart and stubborn. She's ambitious and ruthless. She's exactly what I want.

She pulls away, and I can feel her slipping away again. I can't handle not having her.

"What are you doing?"

"Trying to compose myself so that I don't let you fuck me right here, on the sidewalk."

I kiss her again, pulling her lip back into my mouth, as she moans. "I think you would like it if I fucked you right here."

She blushes. "You're probably right. But then we would both get arrested for indecent exposure, Lily would fuck up her interview, and we would both get fired, our careers over."

I raise an eyebrow. "It would be worth it, don't you think?"

She cocks her head to the side as she stares at me.

"Fine. We'll find a more suitable place to fuck."

"Thank you," she says, happy with her win.

I can see the wheels turning in her head. She grabs my hand and begins pulling me down the sidewalk, desperately trying to get to wherever we are going as fast as possible.

But she isn't the only one with ideas.

I let her lead me down one block before I can't take it any longer.

I grab her hips, and I push her against the brick building while I kiss her again.

"We. Have. To. Keep. Going," she says, kissing me between every word.

"No, we don't."

"We do if we are going to get to my car," she says as I kiss her neck.

I laugh. "We are not going to make it to your car."

She tangles her hands in my hair as she nibbles on my lip.

"Sure we are."

I kiss down her neck again and listen as she gasps.

"There is no way you will make it the two blocks to our cars," I whisper into her ear as my fingers dip inside her pants and beneath her panties to find her pussy already dripping for me. "You will come before I even get inside you. And I can't have that happen."

I pull my fingers back out and lick them while she breathes heavily.

"Fuck me. Now," she breathes.

I grin. I grab her hand, pulling her to the next door. She grabs my face as soon as we enter the building, and her lips kiss me. She can't get enough of me, and I can't get enough of her. She thinks one fuck is going to be enough to get whatever is going on between us out of our systems, but she is wrong.

It's going to take more than one fuck.

It's going to take more than one day.

More than one night.

I'm not sure if I can fuck her enough to get over her.

I keep kissing her as we walk. My hands do naughty things to her body. One hand grabs her ass, and the other pushes her shirt up, needing to feel her smooth skin. We are ridiculous. At least half a dozen people see us as we walk, but neither of us cares.

We continue to act like horny teenagers until we get to the elevators. I press the button, and the doors open automatically. I push Victoria inside and then stop a man who tries to walk onto the elevator with us.

"You don't want to be on this elevator with us, trust me," I say with a wink before the doors close.

I turn to Victoria, expecting her to be blushing from embarrassment but her eyes only deepen.

"Fuck me, Carter."

I press the emergency stop button on the elevator. "I plan to."

I walk toward her, taking my time, while she breathes in and out, in and out. She's terrified—that's what her breathing tells me—but she wants this anyway. She's willing to take the chance.

And I'm going to make it more than worth the risk she feels she's taking.

I stop just as my body touches her. She's leaning against the elevator wall for support, like she can't even stand another second on her own.

"I won't hurt you."

She shakes her head. "You can't keep that promise."

"Sure I can."

"No, because I haven't even had you yet, and I already know that it's going to hurt like hell to have to stop."

"Then, we won't stop."

I grab her arms and push them high over her head as I kiss her against the wall, holding nothing back. She doesn't either. Whatever fear she has disappears the second I kiss her again.

She clutches my jacket and pushes it off my shoulders. I shake it off to the floor. I grab her blouse and rip it open, watching as the buttons pull apart.

"You owe me a shirt."

I laugh. "I think I owe you a lot more than that."

I lower my mouth to her breasts, which are peeking out of her red-hot bra. I kiss over the soft mounds as she pulls at my shirt. She rips my shirt apart, making it known that she is going to fight back with everything she has.

I reach my hands under her damn skirt, find her panties, and tear them down. She grabs my belt, undoes it and my pants, and roughly pushes them down.

Her eyes devour my cock while she licks her lips in anticipation.

"Like what you see?"

Her eyes burn into mine. "I'll like it better when you're fucking me with it."

I grin. "My pleasure."

I grab her bra with my teeth and rip the thin piece of material in the middle of her breasts before I take her newly freed nipple into my mouth.

"Damn it, Carter," she moans as I tease her nipple with my tongue. "That was my favorite bra."

"It might just be my favorite, too," I say before I take her other nipple into my mouth.

She arches her back. Her skin tastes salty from the sweat of being trapped in a tiny elevator with me.

I reach into the back of my pants and pull out a condom. I roll it onto my cock while I continue to tease her. The second I have the condom on, she jumps into my arms, wrapping her legs around my waist while she bites my neck.

I growl as she bites hard, paying me back for the pain I've caused her. I push her hard against the wall as my cock rests at her entrance.

She pulls her head back, so she can look me in the eye as I push my cock just a little into her pussy.

"More," she demands. "Please, God, more."

"I'll give you more than you can ever imagine."

I bury my cock deep inside her as her nails dig into my back.

I growl.

She grins and digs in further. Her mouth grabs my lip and pulls it into her mouth as I fuck her. Her eyes are devious with a gleam of how bad she knows this is but doesn't care. I could stare into her eyes all day if it wasn't for the rest of her body trying to fight for my attention.

Her skin glistens with sweat. Her breasts are swollen, and her nipples peaked. Her stomach is hard, and her pussy is tight as I fuck her.

I try to move slower so that this can last longer, but I can't. Because, every time I do, her moans beg me to move faster. Her nails dig into my back harder. Her pussy pulls me in deeper.

I can't slow down, but I'm going to make this the best sex she's ever had.

I push her harder against the wall as I fuck her.

She gasps before biting her lip.

She doesn't get to hold anything back.

"Let go," I say against her lips before I kiss her again, taking what little air she has away from her.

I kiss her.

She kisses me back harder.

I grab her breasts.

She claws my neck.

I thrust my cock inside her.

She pulls me in deeper.

I tease her clit.

She groans, taunting me with how much I want her in every possible way.

Her eyes sear into mine, and I know she feels it, too. Whatever this is between us, it's more than just sex. But neither of us can speak as to what it is right now.

"Let go of everything," I say, fucking her harder.

She doesn't move her gaze from mine as she begins to come undone. I've never seen a woman come so unashamedly and so passionately as when Victoria comes. Her whole face changes, becoming alive in a way I've never experienced.

She doesn't call out my name. She doesn't say anything. She doesn't need to. Her body says everything. That she hates me. That she forgives me. That she wants me. And that she wants to push me away.

I'm so focused on her that my own orgasm sneaks up on me out of nowhere. It radiates throughout my whole body as I take what I want from Victoria. I explode inside her, releasing everything that I have ever felt for her. Letting go of everything but what I'm feeling right now. A need to have Victoria in my bed every damn night.

"Fuck, Victoria," I growl.

I gently kiss her again, needing to feel her lips more desperately now than before I fucked her.

We stop the kiss at the same time. We stare deep into each other's eyes, trying to figure out what the hell just happened. But neither of us has a clue.

"You should probably put me down," Victoria finally says.

"I don't want to."

She bites her lip and then glances at the doors behind me. "I don't either, but I also don't want an employee to figure out how to open the elevator doors, only to see your bare ass."

I grin. "Why not? I have a fabulous ass."

She blushes. "I'm sure you do, but right now, no one gets to look at your ass but me," she says, winking at me.

I slowly place her on the ground, but I can't take my hands off her. I need to touch her. I need to have her again. I need to be near her. I need her to be mine.

One fuck was not enough. I don't know if I can fuck her enough.

She reaches down and picks up her bra and shirt off the floor. She puts the shirt on and then holds it closed since the buttons no longer work.

I pull my pants back up and pick up my shirt and jacket. I put my shirt on but don't bother trying with the buttons. Then, I entwine our fingers together as I walk to the elevator and start it again before pressing the button for the tenth floor.

"Where are we going?" she asks.

The elevator doors open, and a man is standing on the other side. He smirks when he sees us.

I glare at him as I pull Victoria behind me, trying my best to block his view of my girl.

Except she isn't yours, my stupid mind reminds me.

I glance back at Victoria, who raises an eyebrow at me. I pull her down the hallway and then reach into my pants and pull out the hotel key.

"Wait...you've had a hotel room this whole time?" Victoria says, stopping just outside the door.

I wince. "Yes."

"The entire time? You could have just come here instead of sleeping at Logan's?"

I nod.

"We could have had sex in an actual bed instead of in an elevator?"

"Well, what fun would that have been though?"

She sighs and walks into the hotel room that my assistant got for me just in case. I met my assistant at a coffee shop before I went to Logan's to get the key, but I knew that I wouldn't use it for anything except bringing women here. I just never imagined I would be bringing Victoria here. Now, I can't imagine wanting anything more than fucking her again.

She glances at the clock in the room. "We should clean ourselves up and find some new clothes before we get back to Lily. She should be back soon, and I don't want to get fired for the second time in a month."

I put my hands in my pockets as I watch her try to pretend like we didn't just have sex in an elevator.

"I'll let you shower first while I try to call Logan and see if he can bring us some clothes."

She frowns as she takes a seat on the edge of the bed.

"But then he'd be suspicious of what happened. Let me call around to some local stores first and see if they can bring us some clothes. You shower, and I'll get clothes. Then, we can try to figure out some way to be civil with each other in front of Lily."

With my hands in my pockets, I continue to just stare at her, waiting to see what she will do.

"Why aren't you moving? Shower now. We don't have time for this."

I take a step toward where she is sitting on the bed with her phone, ready to get to work, like she always is. She's a fixer. She fixes things, but sometimes, things don't need to be fixed.

"What are you doing?" she asks, annoyed.

I hold out my hand to her without saying a word. I'm not going to let her push what just happened under the rug. I'm not going to let her push me away.

She folds her arms across her chest. I love her fight, but despite her behavior, I can see in her eyes that she wants to touch my hand again.

"Come with me."

She glances down at my hand but doesn't budge. "Why?"

"Because I want you to."

Her breathing quickens as she looks into my eyes and realizes what I want. That I'm not through with her yet. I'm not sure I'll ever be through with her.

"I..."

"I want you, Victoria. Once was not enough."

I can't see her heart beating wildly in her chest, but I know it is. Her body is flushed, her breathing is fast, and I now know what my body does to her. The same that hers does to me. And I'm not going to spend the rest of the day with her without being able to touch her.

"We don't have time for whatever your deranged mind is thinking."

I lick my lips and watch as her eyes intensely hold their gaze on my lips. She might think she is hiding her feelings well, but I can read her like an open book.

"So, time is the problem?"

She nods slowly.

I pull out my phone and dial my assistant. "Ruby, I need you to get me and Victoria new clothes. Work professional and have them delivered to my hotel room in thirty minutes." I hang up the phone. "Clothes are taken care of."

She swallows hard, realizing that I'm going to win.

"Anything else I need to take care of for you to ensure that we have plenty of time?"

"We don't have time to have sex again. We both need to shower and get ready." She straightens the clothes she is wearing, fighting her grip on her blouse, trying to keep it closed so that I can't see even an inch of her skin.

I hold my hand out again. "Then, we will shower together."

She stares into my eyes and then places her soft hand into mine.

I grab her hand and pull her up from the bed until she is pressed against my body.

"What did you do to me?" she whispers.

I smirk. "I'm making you want me more than you hate me."

I grab her face and kiss her. Hard. This is what she needs to remember how badly she wants me.

Her tongue immediately pushes into my mouth, her hands grab the nape of my neck, and she moans when I stop the kiss.

"That's all you've got?" she teases.

"How did I never notice you before?"

I tuck her messy hair behind her ear even though it's about to get even messier.

"Because you're an idiot."

I grin and grab her hand again. I lead her into the bathroom, hoping to God the shower is big enough to hold both of us.

It is.

I need to remember to give Ruby, my assistant, a raise for getting me this hotel room with a large shower.

As soon as we get into the bathroom, Victoria attacks me. She kisses me like she thinks this is the last time she ever will again. That can't happen.

She rips my shirt off my shoulders and then jumps back, shocked.

"What's wrong?" I ask.

She holds her hands over her mouth as she stares at the mirror behind me. I glance over my shoulder and see the blood dripping down my back.

She spins me around and gingerly touches me on the back. "Did I do that?"

I chuckle. "Yes."

"I'm so sorry. I didn't—"

I turn around and grab her wrists, forcing her to stop touching me. "Don't apologize. You don't get to be sorry for showing me how badly you wanted me. I'm sure I deserved it anyway."

She grimaces, and I know she is still thinking about the wounds she caused on my back. Funny how, a few minutes earlier, she would have been more than happy to give me scars like that on my back. She wanted to rip me apart, but now, she wants to apologize. I think I prefer her wanting to rip me apart.

I lift her up as she squeals in my arms.

"What are you doing?"

I carry her into the shower and turn on the water; it's freezing cold.

She squeals louder. "Carter, stop!"

"No."

I kiss her as the cold water slowly starts to warm up as it pours over our still partially clothed bodies. But it quickly shuts her up, and she forgets about being sorry.

I link our fingers together as we kiss, nibble, lick. The water turns warm, and I kiss down her body, needing to touch every single place on her skin. Her grip on my hands tightens as I take her nipple into my mouth.

"Yes," she moans as I swirl my tongue around her nipple.

I turn her around and push her skirt down her body. I grab on to her ass. Her hands grab on to the shower wall.

I reach into my back pocket and pull out my last condom. *Damn it.* I should have told Ruby to get me more condoms as well.

Victoria reaches back, pulling at my pants, wanting me. Now.

I grin. "Touch yourself."

I don't have to tell her twice. I watch as her hand slips down her body. Little whimpers leave her body as she turns herself on. I'm not sure whether I want to turn her around to get a better view or fuck her right now.

I push my pants down and slide the condom on as the noises she makes get louder and louder.

"You'd better fuck me now, or I'm going to come without you," she says in a snarky voice.

God, this woman.

I grab her hips and push my cock into her pussy as the water continues to pour down on top of us.

"Finally," she moans loudly.

I used to think her voice was annoying. Now, I think it is the most fantastic sound in the world. And her voice gets even better when she is moaning because of me.

"What do you want, beautiful?" I ask, needing to hear more of her voice.

"Fuck me. Hard."

I do. I fuck her harder. She might hate being controlled in the boardroom, but here, she loves when I take over the control. She's begging for a man who can equal her during the day and then take over at night. She needs a man like me, and my dick can't imagine a life without her.

I fuck her until we both come. Until we are both completely exhausted. Yet we haven't had our fill. Too bad we are out of condoms and out of time.

"Can you hand me the shampoo?" Victoria asks.

I take the shampoo bottle behind me, and instead of handing it to her, I squeeze some on top of her head and then massage it into her hair.

"That's not what I asked you to do," she says, trying to sound annoyed.

I don't believe her. She likes me taking care of her.

"You didn't ask me to do this either." I take the washcloth and cover it with soap before I begin to wash her body. I run it over her arms, across her chest, and down her stomach before she grabs my wrist, stopping me.

"Don't."

I smirk. "Why not?"

"Because we will both get turned on, and we don't have time to fuck again."

"We are out of condoms, too," I groan.

She smiles as she rips the washcloth out of my hand and finishes washing herself. "See, the universe doesn't think it's a good idea either."

She steps back and rinses the shampoo and soap off her body. She steps out of the shower while my eyes follow her tight ass.

"I think the universe is wrong then."

She laughs as she wraps herself in a towel. I wash quickly and then rinse off. I turn the water off before stepping out and grabbing the remaining towel. I can see the hint of disappointment in her eyes as I wrap the towel around me.

"How are we going to handle Lily? We can't keep fighting in

front of her, or we are both going to get fired. And I'm tired of getting fired."

"Really? Back to work, just like that?"

She nods. "This was a quick break to try to release some of the tension we were both feeling. That's it. We got it all out of our systems, and now, it's back to work."

I nod. "You're right. That wasn't the hottest sex that either of us has had. That didn't just heighten the sexual tension between us. We are just two people trying to work together. Nothing more."

"Right."

I tuck a strand of her wet hair behind her ear, and her eyes close at my touch as she revels in the feeling. It's the last touch, according to her.

"I won't argue with you anymore."

She raises an eyebrow.

"Fine. I won't argue with you in front of Lily anymore. You can be the lead on the interview since it seems that Lily cares more about what she looks like than what she should say."

Victoria frowns. "And I will let you be the lead on making sure she gets her coffee in the morning."

I smirk but don't argue with her. She wants to be the lead. I'll let her lead. I couldn't care less about Lily anymore. All I care about is finding a way to get Victoria undressed again as quickly as possible. And, if letting her have control over what happens with Lily does that, then so be it.

9

VICTORIA

"Wow, Lily, you look nice," I say as Lily walks back into her office.

"Just nice?" Lily asks, looking from me to Carter.

"You look beautiful," Carter says.

"Definitely beautiful," I say, hating how Carter is looking at Lily a little too much.

But then he looks at me and winks before his hand brushes against my thigh.

I suck in a breath. *Damn it.* This is going to be harder than I thought. I thought we would fuck once and then be done. Carter clearly has different ideas.

I cross my legs away from him and turn my attention back to Lily as I adjust the jacket that Carter's assistant sent for me. It fits well—almost too well. I don't even understand how she knew what size to bring me. I wait for Lily to ask why we are wearing different clothes than when we left, but she doesn't.

"Do you two have your crap together now?"

We both nod.

"Then, let's prepare for the interview."

"Great. Do you have any questions about the interview questions you read through or the direction we want you to try to guide the interview?"

"Nope. Seems pretty clear. I just need to figure out which dress I should wear."

Out of the corner of my eye, I see Carter give me an *I told you so* look. I roll my eyes back at him. Just because he's right doesn't mean he has to be arrogant.

"Well, let's see the choices," I say, hoping I can get some question prep in as she shows me the dresses.

"Yes, I'd love to see you in the different dress options," Carter says, obviously trying to make me jealous by giving Lily attention.

It's working.

I'm ridiculously jealous. It's stupid. I shouldn't be jealous. For one, it's clear he is into me, not Lily. He just fucked me, not her. And, two, I'm not into him. It was a one-time thing. Okay, two-time thing. I shouldn't feel jealous or anything toward him.

I look over at his cocky grin. The only problem is, I don't know how to tell my body that.

———

"You look beautiful," I hear Carter's voice say from behind me.

"Thanks—" I say and then stop as I turn around and realize that Carter isn't talking to me. He's talking to Lily.

I plaster a fake smile on my face. "Absolutely gorgeous."

Lily lights up as she stands just offstage in her dark green dress. She decided on the green one after Carter said it brought out the green in her eyes. I have to agree. She looks gorgeous in it, and it's perfect for the occasion. Just enough sex appeal without looking too sexy.

"You ready?" I ask Lily.

"Of course," she responds.

She looks at Carter like she wants to eat him up. Of course she does. He's hot. Even more so now that he's trying to make me jealous by giving Lily extra attention.

"Good. You're going to do great," I say.

"We are ready for you, Lily," one of the assistants says.

Carter leans forward and whispers something in her ear before kissing her on the cheek.

My heart stops as I watch him with another woman. Even doing something as innocent as kissing her on the cheek. I glare at him as he walks over to where I am, so we can watch Lily on the monitors together.

"I know we aren't together, and you aren't the type of guy who does relationships, but you could at least wait twenty-four hours before you start flirting with another woman in front of me."

His fingers brush against mine. "Someone's jealous."

I roll my eyes. I shouldn't have started this conversation with him.

"Let's just do our jobs and make sure that Lily's interview goes well."

He moves behind me, rubbing my shoulders. "Relax. It's out of our hands now. Now, it's up to Lily."

I fold my arms across my chest as I stare intently while Lily walks out to the couch across from Phoebe. I will not think about Carter again until the interview is over. And, even then, I will only think of him professionally. I will not have sex with him again. The sex might be amazing, but it's not worth the pain I would definitely experience afterward.

The interview starts out pleasantly enough. But then Phoebe turns her questions in a harsher direction, like I was expecting.

"Are you and Phillip still together?" Phoebe asks.

"No, we aren't," Lily says.

I nod. *Come on, you can do this, Lily.*

"So, you are with Jacob?"

"No, I'm alone," Lily says.

I wince when she says *alone*. She's supposed to be coming across as a strong, independent woman. Not weak. Not a woman in need of a man.

"Alone? You don't seem like the type of woman who likes to be alone. You were with two men at the same time after all. I don't believe that there is no special someone in your life right now."

Lily freezes.

I turn to Carter. "She's fucked," I say.

He nods, grabbing the nape of his neck while he watches the disaster begin to unfold.

Think, I say to myself, pacing.

There has to be a way to fix this. That is what I do. Maybe I can find a way to turn the power off and shut down the whole production. Maybe this won't actually air. I might have to sleep with someone, but I can convince them to air an old episode instead of this one.

As I walk, Carter's eyes stay fixed on the screen. Same goes for the backstage crew. Except for the women. Most of the women are either blatantly staring at Carter or sneaking a look. He's attractive. One of the most attractive men I've ever seen. And he clearly has the attention of everyone in the room.

I wanted Lily to have her chance to do this on her own. But she fucked that up the second she wouldn't prepare with me. So, now, she's going to have to do this with a man by her side.

"Carter," I hiss.

He turns toward me with a grin. He clearly thinks I think we should just sneak off and have sex somewhere since Lily is such a lost cause.

"Take off your jacket," I say.

His grin brightens as he takes it off.

I undo the top couple of buttons on his shirt.

"You know I want you, Victoria, but I think we should go somewhere more private before you undress me completely," he says with a wink.

I ignore him as I spit in my hand and then fluff his hair, making it a little messier.

"Roll up your sleeves."

"Why?" he asks, realizing that I'm no longer doing this for sex.

"Because you are about to go on camera."

His eyes widen, but I don't give him time to fight me.

I run over to the production assistant. "Have them go to commercial. We have Lily's boyfriend, and he's willing to go on camera after the break."

The PA's eyes light up as she signals to go to commercial.

"I am not pretending to be her boyfriend," Carter says to me as the hair and makeup team swarm him. "And I'm definitely not going on camera, looking like a slob," he says as the team rolls up his sleeves, like I told him to do earlier.

I shake my head, staring at him with a smile in my eyes. "You are going on camera. You put me in charge of the interview, remember?"

He glares at me. "I am not doing this."

"Yes, you are."

"How is this going to make anything better? How is her fucking three men better than her fucking two men?"

"Because you are going to go on and be charming. You are going to provide a hot distraction for the audience. You are going to say that you used to date Lily in high school. You went your separate ways in college, but you have wanted her ever since. She felt the same way, but you had a girlfriend, and she had a fiancé. But she wasn't happy because the true love of her life was with another woman. She hated herself for not fighting harder for you. But, after everything happened, you realized how much you loved her. You're going to go on and say that everything that Lily did was because she had lost her true love. And, now, you are back in her life. You're going to say that true love conquers all."

Carter searches my eyes. He knows I'm right. He knows that my plan will work. But it doesn't stop him from hating this plan.

He's shoved onstage before he gets a chance to stop it from happening.

I walk back to the monitors to watch. He's charming, attractive, and smart. He offers the distraction that is needed to make people forget about all the bad things Lily did. Clearly, if she got Carter to fall for her, she can't be that bad. The host even falls for Carter. Everyone does.

It doesn't take Lily long to figure out the plan and go along with it. She holds his hand and flirts with him like she really wants him. She probably does. Everyone else watching wants him.

I want him. I just can't have him. I've just sealed my fate by making him publicly pretend to be in love with another woman. He's going to have to pretend to be with her for at least a year until she gets elected. Maybe even for the duration of her term.

I'm not going to be able to do this. I'm not going to be able to watch him pretend to be in love with another woman. It's only a matter of time until the pretending becomes real anyway.

I can't watch this. Not when I'm falling for a man I can never have. I need to get out of here. So, that's what I do. I leave.

10

CARTER

I THROW the door open to Logan's apartment, pissed. I spent the last few hours trapped in a world I never wanted to be in. My assistant, Ruby, thought this is what I wanted. And maybe, for a split second, I thought this was exactly what I wanted. But I was wrong. It was complete torture. And my wants have changed.

I take a step inside and slam the door shut. I head down the hallway to find Victoria.

Logan steps in front of me with a deep grimace, folding his arms across his chest. "What did you do?" he asks.

"What did *I* do? Are you serious? This is your sister's fault."

"I know my sister, and I know you. What did you do?"

"Move, Logan."

"No, not until you talk to me. What happened?"

The bedroom door cracks open, and Victoria stands there, staring at me with wide eyes and a smirk on her flawless face.

I cock my head to the side as I look at Victoria, not Logan. "Victoria decided to make me Lily's new boy toy by pushing me onstage to appear on national TV to discuss a nonexistent relationship with her, effectively deciding what my relationship status will be for at least a year, most likely longer, all so that she could fix Lily's problems after our client didn't listen to us."

Logan turns and looks at Victoria, who confirms my story with the light in her eyes.

I pull out the hotel key card and hold it out to Logan. "Pack a bag, and go stay in my hotel room tonight. It's on me."

Logan looks from me to Victoria.

"You're not going anywhere, Logan. This is your apartment. You are staying here," Victoria says.

I grab Logan's arm, getting his attention again, and I press the card into the palm of his hand. "You owe me, Logan."

Logan frowns. "I don't owe either of you anything. It's more like you both owe me plenty."

Victoria stands next to him, pulling his attention back to her. "I'm your sister. Do what I say, and stay here. Please."

Logan sighs.

"The hotel is the nicest in the city. You can bring the hottest women back to that room. They will think you are a millionaire. Please."

Logan ignores both of us and walks to his bedroom.

I grab the nape of my neck in frustration.

"Some friend you are!" I shout in his direction.

Victoria takes the moment as a win and turns to head back to the guest bedroom. She thinks that, if Logan is here, then we won't fight. That I'll just let her be. But she's very, very wrong.

I go after her just as Logan opens the door to his bedroom with a bag over his shoulder.

I grin.

Victoria's mouth drops open. "What are you doing?" she asks.

"I'm going to stay in Carter's hotel room."

"Why?"

"Because I think you two have a lot of things to work out. I've been in the middle of you two for far too long, and I won't keep doing it."

Logan leans toward Victoria's ear and whispers something that I don't hear before softly kissing her on the cheek. He glares at me as he walks past me, and then I wait until I hear the front door slam behind him before I turn my attention to Victoria. As much as Logan says that he's not picking sides, it sure does seem like he might be picking mine from the way he gave in to my demands.

Victoria crosses her arms and pops her hip out to one side. "Let's hear it. I don't have all day. I need to get to work to revamp our entire plan for Lily, and unlike you, I don't have an assistant I can call to do all my dirty work."

I smirk. "Don't blame me for doing good enough work that allows me to afford an assistant."

She shakes her head. "Don't even act like you do better work than me. I saved us in there."

"*You* saved us?" I run my hand through my hair to keep from strangling her. "You have got to be kidding! You threw me out in front of the cameras because you couldn't come up with anything better. I did all the work. I came up with the stories about Lily and me being together on the spot. I charmed the crowd. I spent all evening pretending to care about a woman. I did all of the real work."

"Fine. You did all of the real work. I'm just taking credit for that work. Just like you did to me earlier."

I hate her. But I also want her. I hate how she's exactly like me. I don't remember her always being like this, but I also love that she is. I'm afraid I've ruined her, turning her heart cold like mine, but maybe I made her that much better.

"I want to fuck you."

She laughs. "I'm not fucking you."

I take a step forward until I can tuck a strand of her hair behind her ear. "You sure about that? I'm pretty sure you've said that before, and it's ended in me giving you the best sex of your life."

"It wasn't the best sex of my life."

"No? Who was better?"

Her eyes dart to the side as she thinks about it. Running names through her head, trying to come up with an answer.

"Andrew. Andrew was better."

"When did you date Andrew?"

"Two years ago."

"Why was he the best sex of your life?"

I see the fight in her eyes. She's not going to give in to me.

"I'm not talking about my sex life with you."

"Because it isn't true. I'm the best sex of your life."

Victoria's face blushes bright red. "Because he loved me. That's why he was the best sex of my life. We were in love."

My heart drops at her honesty. I know I'm the best sex she has ever had. Except for Andrew. Even if he was horrible in bed. Even if he had no idea how to kiss her, how to move her body, how to make her forget about everything. Even if he was horrible, he loved her, and that apparently makes all the difference.

"Well, give me a chance to change your mind. I'm sure you gave Andrew plenty of chances."

Victoria walks past me to the kitchen. She opens the fridge and stares inside at the contents. She starts pulling out a carton of eggs and some bread.

"I'm not talking to you about having sex again. A momentary lack of judgment led to it in the first place. It was just us trying to release our frustrations with each other. That's it. We should talk about what you pretending to be Lily's boyfriend now means."

She turns, and I'm standing right in her way.

She gasps, and I grin.

"What are you doing?" I ask, looking down at her supplies.

"Making dinner."

I grab the carton of eggs and bread out of her hands. "Eggs and toast aren't dinner. It's barely enough food to make breakfast."

She snatches the food back out of my hands. "I'm not that hungry, and Logan doesn't have much food in the fridge."

I grin.

"Will you please move?" she says, clearly annoyed with me.

"You don't know how to cook."

"I do, too. I just don't want to spend time cooking when there are other more important things to do, and like I said, Logan doesn't keep much food in the house."

I nod and smugly walk over to the fridge. I quickly scan it before pulling out some chicken, brussels sprouts, lettuce, and carrots. I move to the pantry and pull out some potatoes. Then, I lay them on the counter.

"Prove it then."

She puts her hands on her hips, like she always does when she is mad and wants to make a point. "No. I don't have to prove anything to you."

"Prove to me that you can cook a simple meal, and I'll stop talking about fucking you. Cook me dinner, and I'll be a good boy and discuss what your crazy plan is now that I'm pretending to date Lily."

She grins. "Fine. What do you want me to make you?"

"Anything that you want with the ingredients in front of you."

She stares at them with wide eyes, not having a clue what to do.

I laugh. "How about some grilled chicken with mashed potatoes, roasted brussels sprouts, and a salad with carrots?"

She nods and then starts opening drawers, pulling out a tiny knife and a cutting board. I take a seat at a bar stool opposite her.

I hold back a laugh as she pulls out the carrots and begins attempting to chop them without peeling off the skin. Each chop requires the full force of her knife in order to make a slice in the carrot.

I laugh. I can't help it.

I get up and walk behind her, placing my hands on hers. "First, you need to peel the carrots."

I reach into the drawer next to her and pull out a peeler. I replace the knife in her hand with the peeler. My hands stay on her hands as I show her how to move the peeler down the carrot. I feel her suck in a breath as I move my head next to hers under the pretext of looking at the carrot.

I reach back into the drawer and pull out a chef's knife. I take the peeler out of her hand and replace it with the knife.

"Then, you can cut the carrot into pieces." My hand glides over hers as I show her how to properly cut it. I can feel her pulse beating faster in her wrist.

I take a step back and let her continue by herself. She takes a deep breath as she adjusts to the emptiness.

"So, what is your grand plan for Lily now?" I ask, leaning on the bar behind her so that I can stare at her body without her judging eyes.

"Um...what?"

I grin. She can act like I don't affect her at all, but it's a lie.

"Nothing," I say, happy not to talk about work right now. It will only make me angry, remembering exactly what she did to me. "You should probably start on the chicken if you want to eat tonight."

She gives me a dirty look over her shoulder.

"Do you want some help?" I ask, crossing my arms.

"No."

She takes the chicken and plops it into a grill pan before putting it on the stove and turning the stove on high.

She walks back over to her cutting board, and after pulling the brussels sprouts out, she cluelessly stares at them.

She takes her knife and chops down hard. The brussels sprout goes flying away from her.

I chuckle.

"I don't like brussels sprouts anyway. Let's just stick to everything else."

I grin and nod while I resist helping her again.

She takes the potatoes, puts them into a pot, covers them with water, and then places it on the stove.

I snicker.

"What?"

"It's going to take hours to boil the potatoes if you don't cut them up first."

"I knew that."

She takes the pot back over to the counter. She pulls the soaking wet potatoes out of the pot and places one on the chopping board. She starts cutting and chops it into tiny pieces.

I shake my head. She's one of the smartest, strongest women I've ever met. *How does she not have a clue as to how to cook?*

I walk behind her again, and she freezes, already anticipating my touch.

"Need some help?" I ask, keeping my distance.

"No," she says stubbornly. She walks to the fridge, searching for something. When she finally finds what she has been looking for, she smiles and pulls it out. "Cheese makes everything better."

I shake my head at her as she pulls out some shredded cheese and pops it into her mouth. She's avoiding my touch, which just makes me want to touch her more.

I have a dairy intolerance, but I'll deal with some stomach cramps in order to get what I want.

I walk over to her and reach into the bag she's holding. I eat some of the cheese as she watches me with large eyes.

She tries to walk around me, but I make sure our hands brush against each other.

She goes back to the cutting board and starts angrily cutting the potatoes again.

"Ouch!" she yells.

I'm behind her in two seconds. My arms are around her body as I take her cut finger into my hands. She's bleeding pretty badly. I pull her hand over to the sink where I turn on the faucet, running cold water, and I begin washing the wound, trying to get the bleeding to stop.

It takes a few minutes, but it finally stops. I turn the water off, and then I lean down and gently kiss her finger.

"All better. I should get a Band-Aid for that," I say, trying to ignore her beating heart and how she looks at me like I just saved her life instead of just healing her finger that would have healed without my assistance.

I sweep past her, but she grabs on to my shirt, stopping me.

She narrows her gorgeous eyes at me as she peers into mine. I don't know what she's doing. I don't know what she's thinking. Her hand moves slowly up my body until it reaches my neck, and then she pulls my neck down until she cautiously kisses me on the lips.

My hands grab her face as I deepen the kiss. Her kisses say so much that I know she would never tell me with her words. They say, *You were right*. They say, *I'm sorry*. They say, *Thank you*.

She pulls away, realizing what she just did, as she wipes her mouth on the back of her hand. She doesn't say anything. She just stands there, looking at me.

"I'll go get a Band-Aid," I say, keeping my promise not to talk about having sex with her again.

I walk quickly to the bathroom, and after searching for a couple of minutes, I come back with a Band-Aid in hand.

"Found one," I say as I return to her in the kitchen.

She hasn't moved an inch since I left. She's clearly lost in her own thoughts when I walk back over to her.

I open the Band-Aid and then take her hand in mine. I place the Band-Aid on her finger.

I lean my head down to kiss her finger again because I can't pass up that opportunity when she grabs my face and kisses me hard again with a force I wasn't expecting.

I stutter backward as I wrap her in my arms and kiss her back.

"I hate you," she says, breaking from the kiss.

"I know." I pull her bottom lip into my mouth, needing this more than she knows.

"And you hate me."

I nod.

"Good. Just so we understand that this changes nothing."

I grin. She's very, very wrong about that. This changes everything. If the first time was a mistake and the second time was a bigger mistake, then the third time is a choice. It means that, despite how mad she is at me, she wants this more.

She grabs my shirt, ripping it open, just like I did to her earlier. Her eyes devour my hard body.

"Damn it," she says.

"What?"

"Why does your body have to be so hot? I've spent a week with you, and I haven't seen you work out once. You shouldn't be this good-looking."

I give her my sexiest grin before I kiss her neck. I grab the hem of her shirt and lift it over her head.

I take a step back to really look at her body. "Talk about hot bodies."

She blushes, and I love it.

"You've been a naughty girl," I say, grabbing her hips and pulling her back toward me.

"Yeah? How?" She moans against my lips as her soft lips kiss me again.

I grab the sweatpants that she changed into and push them down her body. I turn her around and slap her hard on the ass. "You forced me to pretend to date a woman who isn't you."

I slap her again, and she yelps.

She turns her face toward me as she bites her lip. "Does that mean that I have to be punished?"

My eyes deepen with that thought. "Yes."

She bites her lip harder but I realize it's not because I turn her on. It's because she is stifling a laugh.

"You think it's funny that I want to punish you?"

She turns around and swallows as she takes a step away. "Yes."

We both make our move at the same time. She runs, and I chase after her.

She doesn't make it far before I grab her body, pulling her back to me. She grabs the cheese and begins throwing it at me, trying to get me to let her go. I grab her hand and eat the cheese out of it to get her to stop. I suck each of her fingers into my mouth, and she melts.

I should punish her. Make her pay for hurting me. But that would mean not having sex with her. And that would punish me.

Instead, I reach around her back and undo her bra, watching as her plump breasts show themselves to me again. She grabs her panties and pushes them down, and then she's naked, standing in the kitchen.

I groan at the sight of her. Her body is glorious. Her skin is smooth, her boobs are delicious, and her smooth stomach leads down to the tightest pussy.

Her entire body distracts me with thoughts of what I can do with her. Fuck her on the counter, in the living room, or in a bed. Claim her mouth, her pussy, her ass. I want it all.

I look into her eyes though, and I see something there that I didn't see before. Fear.

"Why?" I ask, wanting to know why she pushed me into Lily.

She sucks in a breath as I slowly undo my pants and remove them along with my boxers and shirt.

"Because I was scared."

I grab her and lift her onto the counter, needing her here and now. I need to look into her eyes when she comes. I need to understand everything about her.

My cock hardens as I kiss her. I push against her and then stop, resting my hands on her thighs.

She grabs my face, trying to pull me to her again.

"I need to go get a condom," I say, hating myself for not having a ready stash on hand.

"No, you don't."

My eyes light up at the thought of fucking her without a condom.

I grab on to her and start kissing her again as I push my cock at her entrance. She swats me away.

"What?" I ask.

She looks in the direction of her sweatpants. I grin as I reach down and pick them up off the floor. I dig through the pockets and find a condom, holding it up to her lips.

"Now, tell me, why do you have a condom in your sweatpants? You weren't planning on seducing me when I got home, were you?"

She bites her lip. "No."

I rip the condom open, roll it onto my cock, and then thrust inside her.

"Liar."

Her nails dig roughly into my back as I thrust. I just can't figure out if she is pulling me closer or pushing me away as I fuck her.

She wants this, but she won't ever admit it to herself, let alone me.

I kiss down her neck. I kiss every inch of her breasts, all while fucking her with everything I have.

She moans and groans as she fights with herself, trying to decide if she should hold back or tell me how she really feels.

I'm not going to let her have a choice. I need the truth. Now.

I fuck her faster, pulling more groans from her strong body.

"Why are you afraid?" I ask without having to mention what specifically I'm talking about. We both know I'm talking about Lily.

I grab her hips, pushing harder into her slick opening.

Her eyes shoot wide, looking at me with terror. She doesn't want to tell me. Or maybe she doesn't want to admit the truth to herself, but I need to know.

"What are you so scared of?"

I push harder, holding on to her, not letting her go until I get an answer. I watch her breathing quicken. Her heart is racing, and her whole body is so alive that I know one flick of my tongue over her nipple would be enough to make her come. But I won't let her, not until she answers me.

She fiercely looks back at me, trying to come on her own without my help. Her hand goes to her breast, ready to get herself off.

I grab her wrist, stopping her before she has the chance. She glares at me, but it's just a mask for the fear.

"What are you afraid of?"

"You," she says.

She moves her hips forward to rub her clit against me. It's enough. I feel her pussy clenching against my cock. She growls deep in her throat as her orgasm rolls through her body.

I let go and fuck her hard until my own orgasm pulses through my body. She wants it to be a distraction. She wants me to forget her answer, but there is no way I can forget it.

We both come down, breathing quickly as we stare into each other's eyes.

"Why are you afraid of me?"

"Because you've hurt me so many times before. But those times would be nothing if I let myself fall in love with you. You would break my heart."

I open my mouth, but she kisses me, keeping any words from leaving my mouth.

"Don't make promises you can't keep. You would break my heart. Now that you are with Lily, it can't happen."

The smoke detector starts blaring loudly. Victoria jumps off the counter and races over to where the chicken is burning on the stovetop while I fan the smoke away from the smoke detector.

She thinks I would hurt her. She's right. I've made too many mistakes in the past when it comes to Victoria to be given a second chance. One big mistake comes to mind. When she finds out about it, she will never forgive me. But there would be nothing to forgive if she never found out.

We could start over. This could be our fresh start. It will be complicated with the whole Lily situation, but I've never wanted a woman more than I want Victoria.

"So, I lied. I can't cook," Victoria says, dumping the pan into the sink.

I grin before softly kissing her on the lips. "You are an

amazing woman with plenty of skills, but no, cooking isn't one of them. Good thing I can cook."

She smiles, oblivious to my plan. She's already mine, and she doesn't even know it yet. I won't ever hurt her again. I just have to find a way to prove it.

11

VICTORIA

I STEP out of the bathroom after a long night of sex with Carter. Sex in the kitchen. Sex in the living room. Sex in the bedroom. Followed by sleeping hard in his arms. It was a night I would love to repeat over and over again till the end of time.

I can't though. Today, it has to stop.

I walk into the kitchen to make coffee and a piece of toast, but I quickly change my plans when I see Carter standing in the kitchen with a large grin on his face. I just need to get out of here as fast as possible and grab breakfast on the way.

I walk around the island to grab my briefcase before heading out, but Carter blocks my way.

"Really? This is your genius plan—block my path out of here so that I have to talk to you?"

He smirks and pulls out the barstool at the counter. "My plan is to feed you a real breakfast while I convince you that this can work."

I glance over at the plate. The smells hit my nostrils all at once. Pancakes, bacon, and eggs. I've never eaten so much food for breakfast at one time. But he went all out.

I sigh as I take a seat and begin to dig into the food that Carter prepared for me.

"How is it?"

"Delicious," I say, annoyed that he can cook so well. *It's just pancakes*, I remind myself. But they are the best pancakes I've ever had.

"Good."

I shovel another bite into my mouth. "So, your plan is to cook delicious food for me so that I'll forget about everything else and do everything you want?"

He shrugs.

"It's working," I say with a sigh.

He grins as he takes his fork and tries to get a bite off my plate. I stab his hand with my fork.

"Ow."

"This is mine."

He laughs and leans back. "Fine. But you're mine."

I almost choke on the food in my mouth. I swallow quickly and take a drink of coffee to wash down the rest.

"I'm not your anything, Carter. I'm your coworker; that's it."

"A coworker who has had sex with me how many times now?" he says with his grin that makes me want to do anything for him.

"We can't keep doing this."

"Why not?" He folds his arms across his chest.

"Because of Lily."

"You do realize that what Lily and I have is fake. It's not real. We are just acting to save her career, which was your idea."

"I know. But we can't because, if we got caught together, it would ruin Lily's career."

"We won't get caught. Trust me."

I don't answer. I just keep eating my pancakes.

"What are your other problems with us?"

I push the pancake around with my fork, trying to avoid talking about this.

"I know you like me. The sex is amazing. We could be incredible together. Just give us a shot."

"As I told you before, I don't trust you not to hurt me. We haven't even gone on a real date. All we've done is have sex or fight. You can't build a relationship on that."

He grins, leaning on the counter over my food. "Go out with me tonight."

I shake my head. "We can't. If we got caught—"

"If anyone saw us together, we would just play it off as two consultants on Lily's team, discussing our plan over dinner, nothing more."

I search his eyes, trying to find the asshole that I know is in there somewhere.

"Give me one chance. Go out with me on one date. If you still think us being together is a bad idea, then I'll leave you alone. But, if you enjoy yourself, then we can talk about a plan for us to continue dating. Do we have a deal?"

I try to think about what the cons are to agreeing to such a deal. But I can't, not when he's smiling at me with such hope. I want to go out with him. I want to go out on a date with this fun man. I want to go out with the man who could change my whole world.

"Okay. Just one date."

———

"You shouldn't walk in with me," I hiss to Carter as we walk into the building where Lily's office is.

"Why not?" Carter says, grabbing my hand.

I pull my hand out of his. "Because we can't look like a couple."

He laughs. "You think anyone is paying attention to us? They are all wrapped up in their own lives; they won't notice two people they don't even know."

A young woman comes up to Carter. "Oh my God! Are you Carter Woods? I saw you with Lily on TV last night. I had no idea the two of you were a couple. And that story you told about how you fell in love? It was beautiful."

"I'm glad you enjoyed our story," Carter says, darting his worried gaze toward me.

"I'm Jillian, I'm one of the paralegals for Lily," the woman says, holding out her hand to Carter.

Carter shakes her hand. "It's nice to meet you, Jillian."

"Lily is already in her office, but if you are looking for a place to be alone, there is a restroom on the top floor that nobody ever uses." She winks at him.

Carter smiles. "Thanks for the tip."

I start walking to Lily's office, and Carter jogs after me seconds later.

"Hold up, Victoria."

I slow because I know he will make a bigger scene if I don't walk with him.

"We can't do this. A random stranger from Lily's office noticed you, and we are barely even inside the building. We will get caught if we go on a date."

Carter stops in front of me. "You promised. One date. I will take you to the most hidden restaurant I can find. No one will know. Okay?"

I nod, hoping that something will happen between now and then that will not let me go on that date. Because I know, if I go, he's going to be charming and wonderful and perfect. He's going to buy me flowers and hold my hand. He's going to tell me all the lovely reasons he likes me. He's going to give me his jacket when I get cold and then turn into an animal who kisses me and then fucks me in the cab on the way home. And, after a date like that, I'm going to fall. Completely and fully in love with him because I've wanted him since we were kids. I've wanted nothing more than to make him fall desperately in love with me, but he was always with someone else.

I can't let myself fall in love with him. Because, as much as I want to think that he has changed, I know he hasn't. One day, he will flip the switch again and turn back into the monster I know he has hidden deep inside.

We walk upstairs to Lily's office. I knock before entering. I walk in with Carter close behind.

Then, Lily attacks Carter.

Lily's arms wrap around his neck as she launches at him. And then she presses her lips against his and kisses him. Not a chaste kiss. Not a *thank you so much for saving my butt yesterday* kiss. A real *I want you right here, and I don't care who is watching* kiss.

My mouth falls open at the sight, but I quickly recover. I twirl my hair around my finger, trying to distract myself. I try to force my eyes away from the two of them kissing. But, even if I could manage to somehow tear my eyes away, I could never stop seeing the two of them together over and over in my head.

I knew that sleeping with Carter was going to result in agony. And I was right. I can tell by the look on Carter's face that he is just as shocked as I am about the kiss, that this isn't what he wants. But it doesn't matter. This is our life now. He has to pretend to date Lily. That's the job. And it's going to be the worst pain I've ever felt, watching him with another woman. It doesn't matter that it's pretend to Carter. It's clearly not pretend to Lily.

Carter slowly pushes her back from his lips, and he stares at her with wide eyes. He wipes his lips. "Um...it's good to see you, too," Carter says, backing up toward the door like he wants to run.

I want him to run, too. Forget about this stupid job and just run. I'll chase after him. It can be just like when we were kids, and he chased me all over the playground. Except, this time, when I catch him, he won't push me down. He'll fuck me.

Lily's face lights up. "It's a very, very good day, Carter. The best day in fact."

Carter rubs the back of his neck. "And why is it the best day?"

"Because I have the most amazing boyfriend ever."

"I'm not your—"

A knock on the door stops Carter from speaking.

"Yes?" Lily asks.

"I have a DVD from last night for you," says a small, petite woman when she pokes her head inside.

"Thank you," Lily says, holding her hand out to take the DVD.

Before she begins to walk out of the room, the woman eyes Carter like he's the most delicious man she's ever seen. Lily walks over and takes his arm. She takes the arm of *my* man. I tightly grip my hands together to keep from attacking Lily and claiming Carter as my own. But it's clear that Lily is just as jealous, except she's jealous of a woman who wasn't doing anything other than looking.

When the woman leaves, Lily walks over to the door and closes it. She glares at Carter, still ignoring that I'm even in the room.

"You can't talk like that! There are plenty of people in this office who would head straight to the first reporter if given the chance. If we are going to do this, we have to make it believable. I get in trouble when I don't." She drapes her arm around Carter again. "Plus, I think, after you see this"—she holds up the DVD —"you are going to remember just how good we are together, and we won't have to pretend anymore."

My eyes widen. I glance over at Carter, giving him a *this bitch is crazy* look, as Lily fumbles with the DVD player.

I'll handle it, Carter mouths to me.

I roll my eyes. There is no way he is going to figure a way out of this. Whatever I missed last night made Lily completely smitten with Carter. He was either too good of an actor or...I can't think of the alternative. As much as I thought I could stop this before I had any true feelings for Carter, it's impossible. I've had feelings since we were kids. Kissing Carter, letting him touch me, fuck me made my feelings that much stronger.

"There," Lily says, proud of herself, as the video begins playing. She quickly fast-forwards through the part of the interview where she fell apart.

I should have let the bitch burn out there, I think as I keep my distance. I don't want to see her pretend to be dating my boyfriend.

Boyfriend.

He's not my boyfriend. Not even close. But, right now, I want nothing more than to walk across this room, grab his neck, and show Lily what a real kiss looks like between two people who actually care about each other.

She presses play as she holds out her hand to Carter. I watch his hand. I watch him hesitate for the tiniest of milliseconds, considering holding her hand. It's unfair of me to judge him so closely. I probably even made it up. I'm just torturing myself.

Carter takes a seat at the table near the TV that one of Lily's assistants must have brought in, but he doesn't take her hand. Lily drops her hand with a hint of disappointment on her pursed lips as she leans against the table, ensuring that she can be as close to Carter as humanly possible. I stay standing near the door. I might as well not even be here.

I try to pretend like I don't care. That whatever happens on the TV won't affect me. I know who Carter really wants. Me. Nothing else matters.

But, as they begin speaking, telling stories from high school that I know to be true, it feels less like pretend and more like a real thing between them.

"Give her a kiss," the host says.

My heart sinks. It's just a kiss, but it's a kiss before millions of people on national TV. Something that I can never have. At least, not anytime soon.

I find my legs bringing me forward to watch what is happening on the screen as the crowd eggs them on, wanting them to show their affection in front of them. I walk until I'm standing only a foot from the TV.

I watch as the host asks again for them to kiss, knowing that she's given the crowd enough time to get excited about the two of them. I watch as Carter leans over to Lily and kisses her. I watch his eyes close. I watch his tongue push into her mouth. I watch his hands tangle in her hair. I watch him kiss her like I don't exist.

I don't. It was a lie. I just thought Lily and the world were the ones being lied to, not me.

"That was a genuine kiss, wasn't it, Victoria?" Lily asks.

I nod because my throat is far too dry to speak.

"See? Victoria agrees. We should be together, Carter. Look at us on the screen. We look great together. If I remember correctly, the sex was amazing," Lily says, inching her way toward Carter.

I can't listen to this anymore, or I'm going to vomit or scream or wring both of their necks for letting me get involved in this mess between the two of them.

"I'm going to give you two a minute to figure out whatever is going on between you. I'll be back in a half hour or so to figure out what the plan is," I say, walking toward the door.

Carter pops up, running until he beats me to the door. "Stay."

I shake my head. "You two have plenty that you need to work out."

"Victoria," he says my name.

One word, but I can tell everything he is feeling. Pain, scared, need, lust, sorry. All the feelings I need him to feel.

I scoot past him, walking out the door, telling him how I feel without a word. Betrayed.

I keep walking until I exit the building, until fresh air hits my face. I take a deep breath as I stand outside, able to really think for the first time all day. *I'll take a walk. Just circle the block a couple of times. Give Carter a chance to talk to Lily.*

And then, when I come back, he can talk to me.

I walk briskly, trying to get as much of my frustration and pain out as possible. But walking quickly doesn't help.

I try to reason with myself. I convince myself that their kiss meant nothing. It was just Carter acting, that he wants me, not Lily.

I try distracting myself. I think about Sailor, Amber, my mom. I have hardly talked to any of them since coming here.

I pull out my phone and dial Amber's cell. Sailor isn't out of school yet, but I can call and just check on my sister. I'll call Sailor later in the day.

"Hi," Sailor's meek voice answers the phone.

"Sailor, what are you doing home from school? Are you sick or playing hooky?" I tease, happy. Whatever reason my niece is home, it means I get to talk to her for a few minutes, lighting up my day.

"Amber didn't drive me to school."

My heart sinks. "What do you mean? Sailor, can you put Amber on the phone? I'll talk to you again in a second, I promise. I have a funny story to tell you about an old high school friend of mine."

"I can't. She's asleep."

My heart stops. All my worst fears start flying through my head. That something happened to Amber. She committed suicide. She overdosed. She finally gave up.

"Okay, Sailor. I need to hang up a minute to call Grandma, and then I'll call you right back, okay?"

"Okay."

I reluctantly end the call and dial my mom's number. I give her all the details, and she promises to call 911 and get over there ASAP. But I have to sit here, hopeless. Because I can fix everyone's problems but my own family's.

I shake my head. I can fix my family's problems. I just can't fix my own problems.

I pull up an airline website on my phone and book the next one home. I start walking back to my rental car when Carter ducks out of the building, grabbing on to me.

"I have to talk to you," Carter says.

"I need to talk to you, too," I say even though I don't have time for this conversation. "But it needs to wait."

Carter puts his finger to my lips. "No, it can't wait. I need you to know how incredibly sorry I am. Both of those kisses back there meant nothing. I feel nothing for Lily. Not even the tiniest of sparks compared to what I feel with you."

I smile weakly, trying to pretend I care about his words right now when all I can think about is Sailor and Amber.

"Are you listening to me? I want you, not Lily. I want you, Victoria. I'm sorry about all this mess, but I'm not really dating Lily. It's all a lie. It's all pretend. Lily understands that now. That all we will ever do is hold hands and pretend to be in love and occasionally kiss, although I will try to prevent that at all costs. That woman kisses like I imagine a lizard would."

I zone him out. I can't hear his words. Only focusing on the fact that my family needs me.

"Victoria?"

I don't answer. I just think about if I have time to stop by Logan's to pack or if I should go straight to the airport.

"Victoria?"

I probably should just go straight to the airport.

Carter grabs my neck and waist as he kisses me. I'm caught off guard, but he's desperate to give me everything with this kiss, and slowly, I let him into my world of pain. I let him know how scared I am. As our tongues dance together, I tell him that I like him, too.

He slowly breaks away. "What's wrong?" he asks.

I shake my head and stay in his arms for a second longer. If I tell him what's going on, I'll start crying, and then he'll insist on coming with me. But he can't. He needs to stay here, and I have to go.

"I just have to go. Tell Lily that I quit. That a family thing came up."

And then I walk away from what I know is a man I could love with every fiber of my being. I just don't know if he will still be waiting for me when I get back from fixing my family.

12

CARTER

I SHOULD HAVE RUN after Victoria.

I should have chased her down and forced her to talk to me. Or just followed her until she was ready to tell me what was going on.

But I didn't.

I let her go. And, now, I don't know what's going on. *Is this the end? Is she coming back?*

The hug and kiss she gave me before she left sure didn't feel like the end. It felt like the beginning. It felt like she needed me, but then she just left.

The door to the apartment opens, and I jump off the couch I've been sitting on most of the afternoon, waiting for Victoria to come back. All of her stuff is still here, so she must be coming back soon.

"Victoria, I'm sorry," I say, running to the door.

Logan raises an eyebrow at me as he enters. "Why are you apologizing to my sister?"

I rub the back of my neck. "Because I fucked up."

Logan walks past me toward the kitchen. He opens the fridge, staring at it.

"Aren't you going to kill me for hurting your sister?" I ask reluctantly.

He slams the door shut with anger and rage I was expecting. I know he is going to hit me, and I deserve it. I should never have agreed to date Lily while being with Victoria. Even on a pretend basis. I knew it would eventually hurt her.

"No."

"No?"

He shakes his head. "You might have fucked up, but I've always thought you and Victoria were meant for each other. I think you would make each other better."

I frown. "I hurt her pretty bad. I deserve to be punched or at least thrown out of your apartment or something."

"You're probably right. But, lucky for you, I'm not looking for a fight today."

That's when I realize that the look on Logan's face isn't just rage and anger. It's fear and sadness. Victoria had a similar look before she left.

"What's going on? Victoria just upped and left today, and I have no idea where she is going or when she's coming back."

"She's not coming back."

"Then, where is she? I'll go to her."

Logan's head drops. "Come get a drink with me. I don't have shit in this apartment. Then, maybe I won't end up killing you."

———

"So, what did you do to piss off my sister?" Logan asks after the bartender gives us our beers.

"I made a kiss between me and my pretend girlfriend a little too believable."

Logan laughs. "I really should kick your ass."

I shrug and take a drink of my beer.

"I would, but I don't think Victoria is mad at you because of that."

I raise an eyebrow.

"Okay, I'm sure she isn't happy that you kissed another woman even though it was needed to pull off her stupid scheme. I just mean that she has a lot more important things going on right now."

"And that is?"

"Our sister, Amber, is sick. She has depression. But our idiot mother made it worse by giving her some of her prescription pain killers. Amber overdosed."

"I'm sorry."

Logan takes another long drink of his beer. "Thanks. I just wish I could do more. I can't take off work. I'm horrible with kids. Well, beyond the fun play stuff, I don't know how to actually take care of a kid."

I remember now that Amber has a daughter. I've only met her a couple of times when she was a baby.

"Sailor's amazing, and Amber is great with her when she's well. When the depression takes over again, Victoria always comes in and saves the day. She's lost jobs because of it. Between losing her jobs and getting fired for things out of her control, Victoria has had a hard time with living the life she wants. She usually has to pick up other random jobs just to pay the bills. Her last company made me think it was finally going to make her life work, but then they fired her for no reason. She just can't catch a break."

Realization hits me of where I factor in all of this. I didn't realize what I was doing. I didn't realize I was hurting Victoria. But, now, my problems with Lily seem small.

"What are Victoria's plans now?"

"She checked Amber into a place to help her heal. It will take a few months at least. Our mother isn't much help. So,

Victoria will probably stay with Sailor in San Francisco and try to find another job. She'll survive, just like she always does. I'll fly there any chance I can get and send any extra money I make to help out, but it's never really much help."

"What about her stuff? What about her job?"

"I'll ship her stuff. And job? I thought she said she quit."

"She told me to tell Lily that she quit. I didn't tell her though. I just said she was sick and needed to go home. I told Lily I had some other work things I needed to address and then got out of there as soon as I could to wait for Victoria."

"You need to tell Lily that Victoria quit. She won't come back. She won't pull Sailor out of school or take her away from Amber. She will stay in San Francisco even if she can't find another PR job. She will do everything that she can to fix our family's problems."

I think for a minute, hating that I have to be so far away from Victoria. I don't know when I will be able to see her again. And I know one thing; I can't live without her. I love her. I think I've always been in love with her. I just thought I couldn't love her. That she was all wrong for me.

My mind flashes back to my favorite memory of her. We must have been twelve, maybe thirteen.

———

"Logan," I hiss, poking him in the ribs.

His hand swats me. "Go away. I'm sleeping."

I sigh. It's not even ten o'clock on a Saturday. There is no way he is sleeping. And I can't fall asleep.

I get up from the couch in the basement and head upstairs. Maybe his mom made some food. I walk into the kitchen and open the fridge, but there is no food.

I sigh. So much for that plan.

Music? My ears perk up at the sound of music coming from upstairs.

I creep up the stairs as I listen to the music getting louder along with Tori's voice. I haven't ever heard her sing before, and maybe she will offer me some level of entertainment.

I walk to her door and listen as she belts out Spice Girls. She's horrible, but I don't care. It's amusing actually, how she can sing so confidently. I guess it's because she doesn't think anyone is here.

I throw the door open, planning on embarrassing her. But she doesn't get embarrassed. Her cheeks don't flush, and she doesn't scream in fear.

Instead, she just rolls her eyes at me and keeps on singing into her hairbrush.

I frown. So much for entertainment.

"Sing with me," she says, tossing me a hairbrush.

"No. It's stupid, and you're horrible."

"So? It's fun."

She keeps singing and dancing around the room like a crazy person while I stand, frozen in my spot, with wide eyes.

"You're crazy."

"You're boring."

She walks over to me until she is standing inches away from me. She lowers her hairbrush and says, "Sing and dance with me, or I'm going to kiss you."

"What? Why?"

"Because you don't want me to kiss you. Now, sing and dance with me."

I frown. "I don't know the words."

"Then, make them up." She grabs my hand and pulls me into the center of her bedroom.

She starts dancing again, and I start flapping my arms around.

She smiles. "See? That isn't so hard."

She grabs my hands and spins us around as we dance. As we spin, my world changes. The way she smiles and makes me smile changes everything. Because, for a split second, I wish I had taken the other option. Or at least said both. Because, right now, there is nothing more I want to do than kiss Tori.

I didn't let myself love her because I thought there was no way that she'd ever love me in return. Not after all the cruel things I had done to her. What I did just a few weeks ago is the most savage thing I have ever done. She's going to hate me.

But maybe I'll have a chance if she's already in love with me. Maybe I'll have a chance if I can find a way to fix all the problems I've caused.

"What if she doesn't have to quit?" I ask with a grin.

13

VICTORIA

It's three p.m. I need to leave to pick Sailor up from school. But the bills lying on the kitchen table are overwhelming me. Bills for the house. Bills for electricity and water. Bills to cover Amber's treatment. And that doesn't even include basic things like food and clothes for me and Sailor.

All I can see are bills. And no way to pay them.

What was I thinking, quitting?

I was thinking I needed to be here for my adorable ten-year-old niece. I was thinking that was what was most important. But it was stupid. My mom could have taken care of her for a couple of weeks. Because I can't take care of Sailor if I don't have any money to feed her.

I hear the doorbell ring, but I don't move from my spot. I can't deal with any more nosy neighbors coming to figure out what happened to Amber. I have to find a way to fix my problems. I have to find a way to make a lot of money and fast.

The doorbell rings again and then again.

I sigh. It's probably an annoying kid. I run my hand through my hair. I can feel the tangled knots throughout my head. I haven't showered in three days. I've either been at the hospital with Amber or on the phone, finding a treatment place for her, all while trying to distract Sailor from everything. Basic hygiene hasn't been high on my list.

The doorbell rings again, and I finally force myself up from the table. I need to get up anyway to go pick up Sailor. I trudge to the door, not wanting to deal with any other humans today other than Sailor.

I open the door and fold my arms over my chest, ready to chew out whatever kid is there.

"Carter?" I ask, like I don't know it is him standing in my doorway.

"What are you doing here?" I ask, hating that I'm in sweatpants and an old, ratty shirt. *Why didn't I shower today? Or at the very least, run a brush through my hair or apply some makeup?*

"I'm here because I missed you," he says, carefully choosing his words.

"I missed you, too," I say without thinking, because it's true. I missed him desperately. I missed the obnoxious way that he held me in bed. I missed the way his arms felt while wrapped around me. I even missed arguing with him about everything.

He grins. "Can we talk?"

My phone buzzes in my pocket. The alarm I set to go get Sailor is going off.

"Actually, I have to go pick up my niece."

"Mind if I tag along?"

"Sure," I say, even though I'm not sure at all.

Sailor will ask a million questions about Carter that I'm not ready to answer.

I step outside, closing the door behind me. I lead Carter down to where my car is parked a few feet away.

I climb into the driver's seat, and Carter climbs in next to me. I start driving while Carter stares at me.

"What?" I ask, assuming he is looking at all my flaws and is about to criticize me.

"You look beautiful."

I blush. "Stop it. I do not. I look like a mess."

He tucks a strand of hair, which I'm sure is covered in grease, behind my ear. "You look beautiful because I've never seen you stronger."

I bite my lip. I can't believe he just said that.

"It's true. I never realized how driven you were, how powerful you were, until recently. I'm sorry for that."

I swallow and try to focus on the road. I can't have him saying things like that to me right now. Our life is far too complicated. He has to pretend he is with Lily, and my life needs me here right now. We are on opposite coasts. Anything between us could never work.

"Stop analyzing this."

"I'm not."

He chuckles. "You are because you don't know how this could work. But you've seen my work. You know I'm one of the best fixers in the world. Just one other person might be better."

I laugh. "I'm not a fixer. I can't even fix my own problems."

"I don't know about that. I think you've been doing a fine job so far, but only because you keep putting yourself last instead of first."

I exhale deeply, trying to stay calm. Trying not to get my hopes up that something magical is about to happen. Because that's not my life. My life is one problem after the other. My life isn't easily fixed. My life is a broken mess.

I pull the car over to the curb outside the school to wait for Sailor to come out. Once she gets into the car, then I'll be safe. Carter won't do anything with Sailor in the car.

"Victoria."

One word, and my heart already betrays me. It starts beating for him. Begging me to let him in.

I look at him. His eyes look deep into mine.

"I love you, Victoria. I've always loved you. Since the moment I saw you singing Spice Girls in your bedroom and made me join you. To years later when I realized how many times I'd hurt you. To the moment I saw you again after way too long. There has never been another woman. Only you. I love you."

Everything in my world stops when he says that he loves me. It's something I've secretly wanted since we were kids. Even when he was torturing me, I still wanted him. There was a connection I didn't understand.

I feel a tear slipping down my cheek. I'm literally crying because this man just told me that he loves me. I'm ridiculous.

"Aren't you going to say *I love you* back?" I hear Sailor's voice from behind me.

I didn't even hear her get into the car.

I quickly wipe my tear and turn to Sailor. "How was your day, sweetheart?"

She folds her tough arms across her chest. "I want to hear if you love him first. My day sucked. I could use some good news. I could use another uncle."

I laugh and turn back to Carter. "I love you, too."

He grins as he leans forward and softly kisses me on the lips.

I compose myself before I start driving back home.

"I'm Carter," he says, holding out his hand to Sailor.

"Uncle Carter, you mean," Sailor says, shaking his hand.

I bite my lip to keep from laughing at her sassiness today.

Carter catches my eye. "Definitely Uncle Carter," he says, giving me a wink.

I roll my eyes at him. She can call him whatever she wants, but we are nowhere near ready to make him a real uncle to Sailor.

"So, I have a proposition for you, Sailor," Carter says as he turns around in his seat so that he is looking straight at Sailor.

I raise my eyebrow at him, but I'm not sure that he sees me.

"I'm listening," Sailor says in her sweet voice.

"Your aunt Victoria here has a job in North Carolina. Do you know where that is?"

"Yep! That's where Uncle Logan lives."

"That's right. She has a job that she needs to go back to North Carolina to finish for a couple of weeks."

I furrow my brows, confused as to what Carter is talking about. I quit my job.

"How would you like to go to North Carolina and live with your uncle Logan, Victoria, and me for a couple of weeks?"

"Carter," I say sternly, trying to end this conversation without saying too much in front of Sailor.

"What do you think?" Carter asks, ignoring me.

"I think that would be awesome!"

I look in my rearview mirror at Sailor. "Sailor, you don't need to say yes. It's not fair to you. You would miss school here and go to a different school there for a couple of weeks until I finished working."

"I want to go to a different school."

I frown. "Why do you want to go to a different school?"

"Because there's this boy—his name is Jack—who picks on me all the time. I hate him."

I glare over at Carter.

"What? It wasn't me," he says.

I give him another evil glare, letting him know that, till the end of time, I will blame him for other boys who treat Sailor badly.

"We can talk to your teacher and make sure that doesn't happen anymore."

"No, I need a vacation. I want to go to North Carolina."

I sigh. "Sailor, you need to understand, this wouldn't be a

vacation. You would still need to go to school."

"Whatever. It beats being here."

I exhale deeply, trying to remain calm because my world just got thrown on its head. Apparently, I have a job still. I'm pretty sure I have a boyfriend, whom I can't really date in public, and I'm moving back to North Carolina. I don't understand how any of this came to be or why it's happening. But now isn't the time for questions.

Carter holds out his hand to me, and I take it. I might not be able to fix everything in my life, but I have Carter. Maybe that's enough.

"Now, about that date you promised me," Carter says.

I sigh. "You can take me out when we get back."

———

I said yes to the date just like I said yes to bringing Sailor back to North Carolina with me a few days ago. Now I just have to figure out how to help Amber and I might finally have a chance at fixing my life.

I've spent hours getting ready for our date tonight. I shouldn't have spent five minutes on it since he made it perfectly clear after he showed up at my house in San Francisco that he wouldn't care what I wore or how I did my hair. But I'm making an effort because I'm not sure how many of these dates we are going to get to go on publicly until we figure out a plan to undo my stupid idea of making Carter Lily's boyfriend instead of mine.

I take out my red lipstick and apply it to my lips. I take a look in the mirror. I don't even look like myself. I have so much makeup on. My hair is curled, and I'm wearing a black dress with a few sparkles and heels. Even if anyone recognizes Carter, they won't recognize me.

I hear a knock on the door, and my heart starts racing. I shouldn't react this way to a simple knock, but I do when I know who's behind the door.

I take my time in walking over to the bedroom door—partially because I want to make Carter sweat a little and partially because I have to take time not to topple over in my heels. I open the door while biting my lip.

Carter's eyes light up like he's never seen me before. It's not an expression I'm used to seeing on his face. But it's definitely a look I would like to get used to.

"What do you think?" I ask, popping my hip out.

His eyes travel up and down my body, but he doesn't speak.

"Carter?" I ask, grinning because it's clear from his body that he thinks I look hot.

Sailor pokes her head out from around Carter. "You look hot!"

I laugh. "Thank you, Sailor." I walk around Carter, who is still standing in my doorway with his tongue hanging out. "You going to be okay staying here with Logan tonight while we go out?"

"As long as he's not cooking."

I laugh again. "You're ordering pizza."

"Actually, I made your favorite," Carter says.

I look at him with one eyebrow raised. "You know what her favorite food is?"

"Of course. It's sushi."

"Wow, you do know Sailor's favorite food. But do you really know how to make sushi?" I ask, skeptical.

Carter jogs toward the kitchen. Sailor and I follow. When we enter the kitchen, Carter opens the fridge and pulls out a plate of food.

"No way! You bought that at the store," I say, not believing that he made the perfectly sculpted rolls.

Logan gets up from the living room and walks over. He takes one off the tray and pops it into his mouth.

"How is it?" I ask.

"Delicious. He definitely made them. I was sitting here, watching him make them."

I take one, and so does Sailor.

"Oh my God," Sailor and I say at the same time.

"How did you learn to cook so well?" I ask.

Carter shrugs. "I'm just naturally good at everything."

I playfully hit him on the arm. "Uh-huh."

"Come on. We have a date to get to."

I grin. "That we do."

I bend down and kiss Sailor on the cheek before hugging her. "Make sure Logan doesn't get into too much trouble," I tell her.

She grins. "We are eating sushi and watching *Keeping Up With The Kardashians* all night."

I grin. *Such a mini Amber already.*

Carter's fingers interlink with mine. I glance down to look at our intertwined hands. I will never get used to that.

Carter leads me outside.

"So, where are we going?" I ask.

Carter stops and reaches his hand up to caress my neck as his lips kiss me. My whole body comes alive as we kiss. His lips are all it takes to make me forget about everything other than him.

The kiss ends all too soon.

I laugh when I see his face.

"What?" he asks.

"You have red lipstick..." I run my thumb across his lip to get rid of the lipstick.

He grabs my hand again and pulls me to a limo.

"A limo? Really? Don't you think it will make our relationship more obvious instead of trying to get us to blend in?"

The limo driver opens the door for me, and I climb into the shiny black car. I immediately regret saying anything negative about the limo. I've never ridden in one, and this thing is beautiful. Leather seats, tons of room, and I can have Carter all to myself instead of him being distracted with driving.

Carter slides in next to me. "Want some champagne?" he asks, his voice sounding nervous.

"I'm not really a champagne person."

"Me neither, but it's what you are supposed to drink in a limo."

Carter moves over to the limo's built-in bar. His body looks yummy in his dark suit that somehow looks nicer than the ones he wears for work. He quickly comes back with two glasses and a bottle.

The driver begins driving without a word as Carter pours us each a glass of champagne. I should look out the window to see where we are going, but I don't want to do anything but be here with Carter. We might not get too many other dates like this for a long time, and I'm going to make the most of it.

I hold up my glass to Carter.

He does the same. "To the best night of our lives."

I grin and clink my glass with his. I take a drink.

Carter rubs my earlobe as he studies me.

"What are you thinking?"

"I'm thinking, I'm going to fuck up all my plans for tonight."

"Maybe you should tell me what your plans are, and then I can tell you if they are crap or not."

The limo takes a hard turn, and Carter falls into my lap, losing his drink. Our lips are close together as the electricity between us comes alive. One hand caresses my neck while his other hand is gripping my ass.

I grin because I do know one thing that I definitely want right now. "Fuck me."

Carter's eyes light up at that. He crawls up my body, kissing every inch of bare skin that he can find as he works his way up to my lips.

"You're a naughty girl," he says against my lips.

"A naughty girl who's yours," I say. Every fiber in my body aches for him. Every breath I breathe is because I want to consume his breath. Everything inside me draws me closer to him, wanting him like no man I've ever known before.

He kisses me, and I know it's true. I'm his. I don't want any other man's lips on me.

And Carter is mine. I don't know how to tell him, but there is no way I'm going to be okay with watching him and Lily kiss again. They can pretend to date, hold hands even, but I don't think I can handle anything more than that.

His lips move to my neck, kissing every inch of my skin, while his hand tangles in my hair, undoing all of my hard work.

I groan, loving the combination of rough and soft kisses on my neck and earlobes.

"You have to be quiet," Carter whispers against my neck before he nibbles on my earlobe.

I feel the excitement grow deep in my belly. A feeling that there is no way of containing.

I bite my lip, trying to keep from screaming, but I can't. I moan louder than I did the first time when his lips devour my neck again.

I feel his grin against my skin.

"You're not very good at obeying me, are you?"

I exhale deeply. "You wouldn't be with me if I were."

His fingers travel down my neck and over my cleavage before he grabs my breast. I suck in a deep breath.

"You're right. I want a strong woman who will challenge me on everything."

His hands grab the top of my dress, and I know what's coming.

"Don't you dare," I pant.

He gives me a wicked grin. And then he rips the dress apart, exposing my black lace bra and panties.

"You're going to pay for that."

He sits back on my lap, staring at me. "Oh, I plan on it."

He grabs my hips, and in one motion, he flips me until I'm straddling his lap. I grab his button-down shirt and rip it apart.

He grins. "I figured you would do that. That's why I wore one of Logan's."

I shake my head as I kiss his hard chest.

He groans, and his thick cock hardens beneath me with every kiss.

"This," he says, pointing to my bra, which is extra lacy and sexy compared to my other bras, "I don't want to destroy."

His mouth pushes the bra down, and his lips take my nipple into his mouth.

I dig my nails into his shoulders, careful not to grip him so tightly that I cause him to bleed like before. But he makes it almost impossible for me not to with the way his tongue expertly glides over my nipple and the way his teeth bite with just the right amount of pressure.

He comes up for air, giving me a second to recover, before he kisses me, pushing his tongue deep inside my mouth.

"You can dig your nails in as hard as you want. You can fight with me or love me. It doesn't matter. I love all of you."

I smile. "I don't understand what happened. I don't understand how I can love someone I used to hate with everything inside me, but I do."

He tangles his hand in my hair again and pulls my bare neck

to him, kissing me hard. "It's the sex. I'm way too good at fucking for you not to fall in love with me."

I bite my lip as warm liquid pools between my legs with every kiss. The sex is amazing, and it's definitely something I will never get enough of, but it's not the only reason I love him. It's his charm. The way he takes care of me. The way I know that how hard he used to fight with me is the same fight I know he's going to use to protect me. It's sexy as hell to know that is how badly he wants me.

I grab the waistband of his pants, needing his cock. Now. He's teased me enough. I need to feel him thrusting and pounding inside me. I need to feel fully and completely his.

I push his pants and underwear down, and his hard cock springs free. Carter pushes my panties down while I search in his pockets for a condom. Instead, I find a box. A box I know I wasn't meant to find.

He grins when I hold out the box to him. He takes it from me. It takes me a second to understand what he is doing because it's so crazy that I don't even think of it as a possibility, but when I realize what he's doing, I gasp.

He takes my hand in his. "Victoria, I know this is crazy. I know we've hated each other most of our lives. I know we have gone on a total of one date and that we are currently on it. I know you have your family problems, and I have Lily to deal with.

"But I don't care about any of that. I don't care that everyone else will tell us this is stupid. That we don't even know each other. We already know more than most people do about each other when they get married. And, what we don't know, we will learn. I feel like I've waited all my life for a woman like you, not even realizing that you were that woman all along.

"Forgive me for being stupid, and marry me?"

I bite my lip to keep myself from spitting out an answer that is rushed and not what I actually want. I'm a planner. I plan everything in my life and then watch as all my plans get thrown out the window when reality hits. I didn't plan on Carter. Or any of this. But that doesn't mean I shouldn't say yes.

He opens the box, but I can't look at it. I can't process anything that is happening. This is too fast. Or maybe it's not fast enough, considering we've known each other all our lives. Whatever it is, my mind is too one track focused for me to think about anything other than needing his cock inside me.

I don't have time to look for a condom. I'm on the pill, and he'd better be clean, or I'll kill him later. I grab on to his shoulders as I lower myself onto his cock.

"Fuck me," I whimper against his lips as I look deep into his eyes, letting him know that what I need right now is him. We can talk marriage later.

I move up and down as his hands grasp on to my hips and ass, moving me harder.

"I love you, Victoria," he says as he fucks me harder.

I stare into his eyes, trying to remember this moment forever, as he fucks me harder and harder. Because, no matter what our future holds, this is a beautiful, unplanned moment that we can never repeat. We aren't just fucking. We are changing our future together. No matter if I say yes or no, this moment, right now, will remain with me forever.

"I love you," I say in a whimper as he brings me close to the brink.

"Come, Victoria."

I don't want to come. I want this moment to last forever.

But forevers don't last. Forevers are not infinite. Forevers are only as long as we pretend that our problems don't really exist.

"Come, Victoria. Marry me. Be mine forever."

I dig my nails into his back. I bite my lip. And then I come, pulsing hard around his thick cock, as I let out, "Yes, Carter. Yes."

14

CARTER

SHE SAID YES. Of course, she said yes while my cock was deep inside her as she was coming, but it still counts. And, now, she's passed out against my chest, still almost completely naked.

I don't want to wake her—ever. I want her here, in my arms, forever. Especially if she's naked.

But the driver is going to stop soon, and we need to get dressed.

I lean down and softly kiss her on the forehead. "Victoria, you need to wake up."

She moans and wraps her arms tighter around me in the cutest way possible.

My lips hover over her ear. "If you wake up, we might have time to fuck again before we get there."

Her eyes shoot open.

I grin.

"You're lying," she says, hitting my chest.

"Yes, sorry. You need to get dressed. We will be stopping soon."

"What am I supposed to wear? You ripped my dress, remember?" she says, yawning and stretching.

I point to a bag sitting on the floor toward the front. "I brought a couple of your other dresses for you to change into."

"You knew you were going to rip my dress off me?"

I shrug. "I hoped. It was so fun the first time."

She gets off my lap and grabs the bag. She begins digging through it to find another dress to put on. "You are going to owe me, like, a million dresses by the end of this, aren't you?"

I kiss her on the lips. "More than a million. And there is no *end of this.*"

She nods. "You're right. We should be optimistic."

She pulls out a white dress that I was hoping she would choose and begins putting it on. She looks gorgeous in white, and if I can find some sort of wedding chapel, maybe I can convince her to elope tonight and not wait any longer.

Now that she's said yes, I don't want to wait. I'm a man who knows what he wants and doesn't doubt himself. I know I want Victoria. Forever. And forever needs to start as soon as possible. Tonight, if I get my way.

She pulls a dark blue shirt out of the bag and tosses it to me. We both get dressed while the limo continues driving to our destination.

Victoria runs her hands through her hair. "I look like I was just fucked."

"And is that a problem?"

"It is if anyone sees us together and puts two and two together."

"Let's not worry about Lily or any of our other problems tonight. Let's just enjoy tonight."

"Fine, but I still look like a mess."

"A hot mess."

The car stops, and Victoria immediately goes to the window, trying to look outside.

I grab her hand and pull her back to me. "No peeking."

She pouts. "Well then, show me where we are."

The driver opens the door, and I get out before I hold out my hand to help her out.

Her eyes immediately dart around. "Um...you brought me to a neighborhood? I thought we were going on a usual date, like dinner and movie or something."

I tighten my grip on her hand. "What fun would that be?"

"The normal amount of fun," she teases as I lead her up the stairs to the house.

"Please tell me we aren't meeting your long-lost parents or something. I'm not ready for that."

I laugh. "Nope. I met them years ago. They were horrible people. Not quite as horrible as my foster parents, but still pretty bad."

"I'm sorry," she says, stopping, her brows furrowed in a look of genuine concern.

I stroke her cheek. "Don't be. I'm not. Family has never been important to me."

She frowns and fidgets with the hem of her dress. "Then, why do you want to get married if family isn't important to you?"

I sigh. She's going to ruin every surprise I have planned for her today. "Just come inside with me, and then we can talk."

She wants to fight. I can tell from the fierce stare I'm getting, but she relents and follows me up the stairs to the front door. I reach into my pocket and pull out the key.

She inquisitively looks at me, but I don't answer her unspoken question yet. I put the key in the door, unlock it, and push the door open.

I hold the door open for her, and she walks inside the large house.

"Wow, this house is beautiful," Victoria says, looking at the quaint home.

I take her hand and lead her to the back of the house, out the

French doors, and out onto the large patio. Twinkle lights hang overhead, already on, and large trees and flowers cover most of the yard.

"It's so peaceful out here," she says, standing on the patio, looking out over the large backyard, which has a pool where I plan on fucking her later.

I get down on one knee and pull out the box that I snatched back up after Victoria found it in my pants pocket.

She grins this time, unlike the last time when I took her completely by shock. I wouldn't change it for anything though. I loved hearing her say yes with my dick inside her.

"Victoria, I love you. I don't have any family, and I never thought I needed one. Not until you and Logan. Logan has always been a brother to me, but for some reason, I could never make you my sister. That's because I'm meant to be your husband, not brother. I already think of Sailor as my niece. And Amber as a sister. I want us all to be together to figure out whatever our problems are—together.

"This house is ours if we want it. It's big enough for us all to share when we are in town. I think, after Amber recovers, it would be good to get her out here to live with Logan and us when we are here. This house is so peaceful and beautiful.

"But, if that's not what you want, then I will find another solution. Because your family is my family now, and I will do anything for them.

"Now, I've already asked you this once, albeit not in the most romantic way."

I open the box, revealing the large diamond. "Marry me."

"Yes," she says behind her laughter. "It's crazy, but I'll marry you."

I put the ring on her finger before grabbing her in my arms and twirling her around.

"You have to promise me some things though if I marry you."

I laugh, putting her down but not out of my arms. "Of course you have demands in order for you to marry me." I sigh. "Let's hear them."

She thinks for a minute with a goofy smile on her face that I love. I love that she has demands. I love that she doesn't just say yes without having her own needs met.

"One, we get this house, no matter if my family wants to live here with us part-time or full-time or whatever. I love it."

"Done."

"Two, you have to promise me that you will respect my decision if I decide not to have kids. I don't know what I want right now. I love Sailor, but I already have enough people to take care of in my family. And I love my career. I'm not ready to give it up yet."

"Done."

"Three"—she twists her fingers deep into my hair—"you will never stop fighting with me."

I frown. "You want me to fight and argue with you? Seriously?"

"Yes, fighting with me makes both of us better. It ensures that we will never get bored. It will push us if we have to compete over the same clients in our careers."

"Or we could work together?"

She laughs. "How well has that been working for us so far?"

"Good point."

"Promise me?"

"We will have a lifetime of fighting and arguing about everything."

"Good."

"Are you done?"

She smirks. "You think I have only three demands?"

"I think I want to kiss you, so you'd better hurry up."

"Four..." She takes her time, thinking really hard, while my patience for not being able to kiss my fiancée grows strong. "Four is, you have to take me down to the pool and fuck me."

I grab her ass and lift her up. I begin running down the stairs toward the pool. "Thank God we think so much alike."

"Shut up, and kiss me."

Her hands grab my neck as she forces my face forward to kiss her. Her tongue pushes deep inside my mouth as I push back equally with my own tongue. We are perfect equals who will challenge each other in life. I want exactly what she said she wanted.

I try to pay attention to where I'm walking. But I can't focus on anything but her lips, her tongue, her body. I need all of it. Fast, slow. Hard, gentle. I need her in every way possible.

I take another step and don't feel anything beneath my foot. I try to lean back to keep from falling, but I can't stop us once we've started moving. We fall into the water, still clothed and still grasping on to each other, desperate for a kiss.

We come up for air at the same time. I expect her to be pissed or to be full of giggles over what just happened. Instead, we continue kissing right where we left off. Deep, passionate, *I will never let you go* type kisses.

I grab the hem of her dress and pull it up over her head until it is off her body.

"Damn, you look hot," I say, biting my lip, as I stare at her in the pool with the twinkle lights shining down on her.

"And you look far too clothed."

I take my jacket off and throw it onto the side of the pool. She helps me remove my shirt, and then I push my pants and boxers off, not caring if they make their way out of the pool or not.

"Better?" I ask.

"Much," she says, undoing her bra and pushing her panties off before she dives under the water.

Damn it. I forgot how much of a good swimmer she is.

I dive under after her, chasing her across the pool. She stays under the water when I finally catch her. She used to swim, so I'm sure she can hold her breath for hours. I can't.

I kiss her hard, convincing her to come up for air to get another kiss. She does. When we get to the surface, I grab her and push her against the wall of the pool, kissing her hard as my cock pulses at her entrance.

"I want every day to be like this," she whispers against my lips.

My cock thrusts inside her, stretching her wide. "It will. Always."

I fuck her hard against the edge of the pool. And she fucks me right back. As much hate as we had toward each other, I wouldn't change anything because it created this perfect kind of love where we are truly equals who fight for what we want in this relationship.

———

"Thank God you brought extra sets of clothes," Victoria says, naked, as she climbs out of the pool to scoop up our clothes.

I frown. "I disagree. I think it would have been better if I hadn't bothered with clothes. I much prefer the view when you're naked."

She laughs and scoops up our wet clothes. My phone falls out of the jacket pocket and bounces on the concrete.

"Sorry," she says, wincing.

I laugh. "The water probably destroyed it anyway."

"I'll try to fix it," she says, running into the house with my clothes and phone, which I'm sure is unfixable. I stay in the pool, planning on doing a couple of laps and then going inside to try to convince Victoria to have sex in one of the rooms in the house before I take her to a late dinner.

I do a couple of laps, loving that this could be my new life. Married to Victoria. Waking up to sex, then a couple of laps in the pool, and then off to my dream job. *How could my life get any better?*

On my third lap, I feel something hard hit my head. I stop swimming and look up to see Victoria still dripping wet but with a new dress on, which is getting wetter by the second. But that isn't what matters. I look at Victoria's face, and I know something is wrong.

"What's wrong?"

She holds out my phone.

"I told you it wasn't fixable."

She shakes her head, looking at it. "It works just fine."

I raise an eyebrow, not believing that the phone works.

"Your assistant, Ruby, called."

"Okay," I say, not understanding why Ruby called or why it would make Victoria upset.

"You got me fired. All those times I thought I had done something wrong. I hadn't gotten enough clients. I hadn't worked hard enough. I'd worked too hard. I'd demanded too much money."

I shake my head. "No, let me explain."

"Every time I was desperate to do a job I loved to take care of my family, you took it away from me. Every. Single. Time."

Victoria's face is bright red, her nostrils are flared, and she is trying to hold back the tears in her eyes.

"Victoria, it wasn't like that."

She throws her hands up. "How was it then? Tell me because I don't understand it. Were you that threatened by me? Is that why you did it? You hated me that much? Has this all been just one big game to you? Or were you pretending to love me to gain some forgiveness?"

The tears fall freely now, mixing with the anger steaming off her cheeks.

"Victoria, I'm sorry. I—"

"You're sorry that you are actually in love with Lily and just pretending with me?"

"No!" I swim to the edge and jump out of the pool, running toward her. "I love you, Victoria. That's always been the truth. Lily is nothing to me."

"Then, what?"

I take a deep breath. "I had to win at all costs. That was always who I was. When I heard there was a new woman in the game who was starting to beat me out for some clients, I felt threatened. I couldn't allow you to win. So, I got you fired."

"But it was me! I know we used to hate each other as kids, but really? You would do this to me? To Logan?"

I wince. "I didn't know it was you."

"How could you not?"

"I always thought of you as Tori, not Victoria. I never connected the dots until—"

"Until I said to call me Victoria, not Tori?"

I nod. "I was going to tell you."

She laughs harshly. "Sure you were." She throws the phone at me and then begins running inside.

"Victoria, wait! Let me explain more. I was an ass. I would do anything to win. I didn't care about anyone. That was before I knew you and loved you. I'm sorry."

I chase Victoria through the house and then outside. I don't care that I'm naked. I can't just let her go.

I catch up to Victoria just as she is about to climb into the limo.

"Please, just stay. Let's talk. Tell me how I can make this better."

"You can't."

"I'll do anything."

She shakes her head. "No, you won't. You're selfish and cruel and savage. You won't do anything for me if it means having to give something up for yourself."

I don't have words. I can't come up with anything to say that will make her stay. Nothing that will make this any better. I can't fix this. I don't know if I'll ever be able to fix this from the look on Victoria's face. So, I let her go. I watch her climb into the limo and close the door. I watch the driver drive her away while I stand in the driveway, naked.

———

"You look like death," Lily says to me when I walk into her office a week after Victoria ran out on me.

"I've been sick for a week. What do you expect me to look like?"

"Happy, cheerful, sexy, ready to work."

I groan. "I don't think I can be any of those things ever again."

She laughs. "Oh, stop being so dramatic, Carter. You have a cold. You'll survive."

"No, I won't."

She rolls her eyes. "I'll have to have my makeup team work on you, too, to make sure you look good for our appearance tonight."

I wince from just thinking about it. "Lily, you know, I've been thinking."

"Shh. You're sick," Lily says, sitting next to me at the table, stroking my hair. "You don't need to worry about any of the plans. Victoria got everything covered before she had to leave."

"What do you mean, she left? She quit?" I ask, annoyed that she isn't even going to show up to work. I thought this was my best chance at seeing her since my best friend had decided to take sides after all—choosing Victoria's, not mine. So, I haven't been able to get into his apartment all week.

"She said she had family things that she had to deal with and, unfortunately, couldn't continue. Don't worry; she came up with an excellent plan for going forward, and I paid her well for her idea."

I frown. I don't like this at all.

I sit up, straighter, swiping Lily's hand off my head. "What exactly is her plan?"

Lily grins. "I'm not going to tell you."

My face turns bright red. "Why not? Shouldn't I know the plan that I'm supposed to execute with you?"

"No, all you and Victoria did was fight. If I tell you her plan, then you will try to change it, and it's perfect as it is."

I narrow my eyes as I stare into Lily's eyes, trying to figure out what the plan is, but I see no hint in her eyes other than seeing that she is happy.

"Don't worry; I'll pay you well, too," she says, petting me again.

I grab her wrist, needing her to stop touching me.

She reluctantly pulls it away, getting the hint. I stand up and walk toward the door.

"Where are you going?" Lily asks.

"To get ready for tonight. Apparently, I'm only a hot body that needs to look good for our TV appearance tonight."

She smiles. "Try to sleep. It will help with the circles under your eyes."

I nod, giving her a fake smile before I leave.

I don't have a plan. Not yet, but I do know Victoria. I know that she needed this job, so she convinced Lily to pay her a large amount of money for whatever her plan was. I also know that, after I hurt her, she will retaliate. So, whatever the plan is, it isn't going to be in my favor.

But I also know that I still have a chance with Victoria if I can form my own plan. She thinks I'm selfish, cruel, and savage. She's probably right. But it doesn't mean that I don't love her and that I won't do anything I can to keep her. She's giving me another chance by retaliating and getting her revenge. She's showing just how selfish, cruel, and savage she can be. I'll let her. I deserve whatever revenge is coming my way. It will equal the score. And then maybe we can get back to the love part after we get all of our hate out.

15

———

VICTORIA

I HAVEN'T SEEN Carter in a week. But I'm going to tonight.

I squeeze my hands into fists and then release them.

I try to replay Sailor's voice in my head. *You look great.* I repeat those words over and over. *I look great, and tonight, I'm going to make Carter suffer.*

He's going to hate me by the end of tonight and also want me more than he's wanted any other woman. He's going to feel pain when he realizes that I'm not here for *him*. I'm here to make him pay for all the years of pain he has caused me.

I walk backstage of the television show that Carter and Lily are going on. I walk right up to both of them, trying to squash any nerves about still having any feelings toward Carter. I can't have any feelings. He hurt me; now, I'll hurt him. That's all we will ever be to each other.

"Hello, Lily. Are you ready to go tonight?" I ask.

Lily throws her arms around me. "Victoria, it's good to see you! I wasn't sure if you would make it."

I grin brightly at her. "I wouldn't have missed it."

"I'm very sorry to see you go. You really are the best."

"Thank you, but you won't need my services anymore after

tonight. Your crisis will be over, and you will be able to focus on running an effective campaign."

Lily smiles. "You're right, but if I need someone to handle a crisis in the future, I'm calling you."

"Hopefully, you won't need to."

I glance over at Carter, who is intently watching me but doesn't say anything. I don't say anything to him either. I just stand there, letting him wish that he had treated me like I deserved. Because I'm going to make sure he'll miss my body.

His eyes travel over my body, like I knew they would, soaking in his last glimpse of me. He takes in my legs, which look curvy in my dark jeans and high heels. He takes in my white spaghetti strap top, which has plenty of cleavage and shows off my arms. And then he settles on my face. My hair is curled in loose waves, and my makeup makes it look like I'm going out tonight to pick up a guy. And I might just do that. I could use a night to forget about everything.

"You're on in five," one of the assistants says to the couple.

"Good luck," I say to Lily. Then, I give Carter one last glare before I walk over to the monitor to watch Carter's life end.

They are announced, and I watch them walk out, hand in hand. All smiles for each other.

I feel the stabbing in my heart. *Damn it.* I'm not the one who is supposed to feel pain. He is.

They take a seat in the chairs, and the host begins asking them easy questions at first. They both make jokes and laugh.

And then the host says the words that I planted. The words that I'm here to watch. "I hear that the two of you have some big news to share."

Lily holds tighter on to Carter's arm, leaning in like she is really in love. She probably is—or at least, what she thinks is love. "We do have some exciting news."

"Care to share?" the host asks excitedly.

Lily holds out her left hand, proudly displaying the engagement ring that Carter used to propose to me a week ago. "We're engaged!"

I carefully watch Carter's expression. He's surprised. He raises an eyebrow for a split second when he sees it, and his eyes are a little wider than usual as he stares at the ring on Lily's finger instead of mine. But he quickly recovers from the surprise. What he doesn't recover from is the pain. I know he was expecting me to do something, but I don't think he was expecting that. He looks away from Lily and over to the backstage area where I'm standing, off camera. I look away from the screen to look at him with a smirk. He deserves this. He deserves the pain. He deserves to suffer, being her fiancé. If I get my way, until death do they part.

"Tell us how you proposed," the host asks Carter, forcing his attention back to the interview.

"Oh, it was so romantic! We were in a limo, and...well, things got steamy," Lily says, fake blushing. "But, Carter, you should really tell the story."

Carter takes a deep breath. "I had rented a limo for the night because I wanted everything to be perfect. And it was. We started kissing. Then, one thing led to another, and our clothes were off. She was digging through my pants, looking for protection, when she found the ring. I proposed. But she was more worried about being with me than being very clear with her answer.

"The limo driver kept driving to our destination—a home that I bought for us to start our life together as a family. And I proposed again on the deck of the house, under twinkle lights and the stars. She said yes."

"Oh my God, that is a romantic and steamy story," the host says.

Carter smiles, but it's fake. He hated retelling that story and replacing me with Lily. It hurt. My job here is done.

I walk toward the exit, feeling the weight of what I just did hit me harder and harder with every step. I just hurt a man whom, despite everything, I'm desperately in love with. A man who, minus a few flaws, is perfect for me in every way. I just ruined my chance at happiness with him.

I throw the door open and step outside, wrapping my arms around myself, trying to comfort myself, as I walk the two blocks to the nearest bar. I stop outside the bar and turn around, hoping that, just like in the movies, Carter will be there, running after me, about to give me some fantastic speech that will make me feel like we can be together. But he's not there. No one is.

I'm all alone.

I need to get used to it. This is my life now.

16

CARTER

THE INTERVIEW ENDS, but my relationship with Lily is just beginning thanks to Victoria.

She hurt me.

It felt like she ripped out my heart and then tore it into tiny little pieces. I couldn't breathe. I couldn't think about anything other than the fact that she gave her engagement ring to Lily. It was a cold move forcing me into a fake engagement with Lily.

And I deserved every ounce of the pain she caused me. That much I know. Up until a few days ago, I have spent my whole life hurting Victoria. When we were kids I did it because it was fun and I was deflecting from my own pain, but as we got older I realized it was because I cared about her, but I was never good enough for her. But I couldn't let anyone else have her.

I couldn't let her beat me because that would only reinforce that I'm not good enough for her.

But now, neither of us win. Because we can't be together.

I look over at Lily who is showing off her ring to everyone that will look at it backstage.

I do have a choice. I can tell the truth. I can let everyone know that Lily's and I's relationship is a farce. I can ruin my career along with Lily's and probably Victoria's. I can be selfish in order to have a shot with Victoria now.

Or I can do my penance. I can continue to pretend to have a relationship with Lily. Follow the plan that Victoria set in place and then try for a relationship with Victoria afterward.

I'm not sure I like my odds of either option working out. I'm a fixer. I fix things, but I have no idea how to fix my relationship with Victoria.

I duck out of the back door while Lily holds everyone's attention. Apparently, no one cares about the guy in all of this. I don't know what choice I'm going to make, I just know I need to talk to Victoria. If I can talk to her and see where she is at, then maybe I will know which choice I should make.

I run down the street hoping that she is still nearby. She would have wanted to stay and watch the interview. I know she would want to see the pain she caused burned into my mind. But I'm not sure where she would go afterward.

Alone. She would want to be alone. I look into the bars as I walk and stop dead in my tracks when I see her sitting at the counter of an almost empty bar. I grab onto the handle of the door as I watch her talking with the bartender.

I want to throw the door open and run over to her and carry her out. I want her to be mine. I want her to want me. I want her to forgive me for all the horrible things I've done. But I know looking at her now that I can't. She's not mine.

The only way she will ever be mine is to let her go. Show her that I've changed. That I would put her first above my own needs. And the only way to do that is to do what she wants. I have to pretend to be with Lily.

I just have no idea how to earn her forgiveness for all the pain I've caused her.

I take a step back and think about my options. I don't have many. I duck into the next restaurant and ask the hostess for pen and paper. She hands me a napkin and her pen uninterested in what I'm doing.

I scribble down a note to Victoria and then give the hostess a twenty to deliver the note to Victoria. I stand outside as the hostess enters, but disappear before Victoria has a chance to come after me.

I can't talk to her today. I can't talk to her tomorrow. I can't talk to her next week. It's going to take a long time to undo the damage that I've done. But I'm willing to wait. However long it takes. A year. More.

I want her to wait for me. I want her to think only of me. But that's not fair. She shouldn't wait. She should live her life while I do everything I can to make it up to her. Because she deserves to be happy. Even if it means without me.

———

It's been six weeks, twelve hours, and fifty-two seconds since the last time I saw Victoria. And every single one of them has been a living hell. I hate my new life. I hate pretending to care about a woman that I don't. I hate being paraded out to interview after interview. To event after event like a show pony.

I hate running my company from a distance, not really able to take on new clients because it interferes with the work I'm doing with Lily.

But most of all I hate not hearing from Victoria.

I walk into the bar where Logan works with Lily draped all over my arm. The new shiny ring that I bought her to replace Victoria's ring sparkling brightly on her finger. I couldn't really change the style of the ring after she showed it on national television, but I couldn't spend a year with Lily watching her wear the exact ring that I had used to propose to Victoria with. It hurt too much.

One year. That's how long I promised Lily I would keep up this farce. Long enough for her to win, and then we would come up with a reason that I leave her. A drug problem. I cheat on her. Something. I just have to survive one year and then I'll be free.

I spot Logan behind the bar and walk over to it with Lily clawing at my arm the whole way. Our bodies don't sync together like Victoria's and I's do, which makes it almost impossible to walk together naturally. We make it to the bar and I pull out a stool and take a seat not bothering to help Lily with her stool.

She huffs beside me as she has to pull her own barstool out and take a seat without the help of her charming fiancée.

Logan smiles as he walks over to us and leans on the bar.

"Hey, Carter! It's good to see you in person man. I'm not used to having to turn on my TV in order to see my best friend."

I exhale. "Sorry about that. I'll try to stop by more now that things have settled down a bit."

"Can I get you something to drink?"

"Beer," I say.

"Oh good of you to look at me," Lily says when Logan finally gives her attention. "I'll have a white wine."

He gives me an *it sucks to be you* look and then turns to get us our drinks.

"You don't have to be such a bitch to everyone you know. Logan and I are best friends, be nice."

She smirks. "You and Logan are no longer best friends. I own your ass for the next year and I don't want you hanging with a slum like him. It's not good for our image as a couple. So you better say your goodbyes now."

Her phone buzzes in her purse and she pulls it out and answers in her annoying high-pitched voice before giving me an *I'll be right back* look and gets up to take the call away from me.

I sigh. I don't know how I was ever able to stand her when we dated in high school. Probably because we just had lots and lots of sex and very little talking. Probably because she was just a distraction from my best friend's sister that I could never admit that I had feelings for.

Logan returns with my beer and Lily's wine. He sets them down on the bar.

"Where did the evil witch go?"

"Phone call," I say drinking down half the beer.

Logan laughs and pulls out two shot glasses and fills them both with whiskey. "I think you could use one of these." He slides me one of the shots and takes the other in his hand. We clink them together and down the shots.

"So what did you really come here for, because it wasn't to see me," Logan says.

I frown. "I did want to see my best friend, but..."

"But you want to know how Victoria is doing?"

I nod. "But I shouldn't know. I won't be able to keep doing what I'm doing if I know too much about Victoria."

Logan laughs. "What are you doing? Because it seems like you are making the biggest mistake you've ever made."

"I'm paying for all of the mistakes I've made with Victoria."

"You're going to be paying for a long time, you made a lot of mistakes when it came to Victoria."

"I know. I'm just hoping that I can pay for them within the year. And I have to keep working for Lily. It's the only way that I and, more importantly, Victoria keeps getting paid for the job that she did fixing Lily's mistakes."

I glance to the lobby where Lily is pacing on her phone. She will be back soon and who knows when I'll get a chance to talk to Logan again face to face.

"How is she? I don't need to know all of the details. I just need to know that she has more than enough money to take care of the family. And that she is happy."

Logan rubs the back of his neck and I can see in his eyes that he wants to tell me something, but is not sure if I want to hear it.

"She's happy."

I stare at my glass of beer, watching the bubbles fizzle as I try to be good. She's happy. I don't need to know more.

"What do you want to tell me?" I ask, not looking up at him because I hate myself for asking about her.

"It's not mine to tell. If you want to know more about Victoria, you're going to have to ask her yourself."

"Damn it, Logan! Just tell me. Tell me she's dating someone else." I grip the glass too tightly and watch as it crushes in my hand. Little pieces of glass stick to my hand along with the beer.

Logan shakes his head at me before he walks over and grabs a wet rag, tossing it to me to clean up the mess.

"Victoria isn't going to want you if you are a jealous mess. You were the one that decided this was for the best. You decided that the only way to get her back was to put in the work. Then do it.

"And in the meantime, Victoria is going to live her life. She deserves to be happy. She takes care of all of us. She may be the youngest, but she somehow was always the one that was strong enough to deal with all of our crap. We wouldn't be here without her.

"So do the work man, and when you are done, you'll have Victoria's forgiveness."

"And her heart?" I ask, swallowing hard.

Logan shrugs. "You'll either have it or you won't. But either way, Victoria will be happy."

"I need a napkin and a pen."

Logan frowns as he moves down the bar and grabs me a napkin and a pen from his pocket and places them on the bar in front of me.

I start scribbling on it.

"What are you doing?"

"I'm starting at the beginning and writing an apology for every time I've ever hurt her."

I stop writing and Logan snatches the napkin out of my hand and starts reading.

"I'm sorry for stealing your only barbie from you when we were little. It was mean. I was six and didn't know better, but it still isn't okay. I watched you cry and I didn't give it back. I'm sorry," Logan reads. He glances at me. "You really are starting at the beginning."

I nod.

He flips the napkin over and I try to snatch it back before he reads the other side.

"I know you are too old for barbies now, although I'll send one for Sailor to play with. But for you, I need you to do something for me. I miss kissing you, desperately. Your lips are what I dream of every night. Don't let your luscious, fuckable lips go to waste. Kiss a stranger, or a lover. Kiss someone for me."

Logan stares down at me when he finishes, completely silent. "You really love her, don't you?"

I nod. "I think I've always loved her. I just didn't understand how to love someone. I'm still not sure I do. My family taught me how to treat people like shit. And the only way I got out of the situation was by having a ruthless career that took down anyone and everyone in my path. Even Victoria."

"Why a napkin?" Logan asks, offering me no comfort. He doesn't say that I already know how to love, which only makes me realize that taking this time is my only chance at figuring out exactly how to love.

"Because it's what I wrote on and gave her the night Lily announced our engagement on television. The night Victoria decided to get her revenge. I could write on paper, but writing on napkins lets her know that I'm thinking about her always.

Even when I shouldn't. Even when I'm just having a drink or grabbing a bite to eat. I'm not just sitting down to write a long note in order to try to win her back when it's most convenient for me. I'm always thinking of her." Always, forever, I'll never stop.

17

VICTORIA

I HOLD the envelope in my hand as I walk out onto the balcony.

I lean over the edge of the railing and take a deep breath as I stare at the envelope addressed from Carter in my hand. I turn it over and over again deciding if this will be the one that I finally just toss into the pool instead of opening and reading. Every time I receive one, which is at least once a week, sometimes more, I do this. I tell myself I'd be better off just tossing them out and forgetting about Carter, but I can never actually do it.

As much as I want to be over him, I'm not. I bought the house that he proposed to me. I will never stop thinking about him. Never stop loving him. But I need to get over him.

I look down at Amber and Sailor playing in the pool together. They are happy. Happier than I've ever seen them.

If I'm thankful for one thing about Carter it was his idea to buy a house that we can all live in. That's what I was trying to do in San Fransisco, but it was too close to our mother. Too close to our pasts that we needed to escape. And it didn't include Logan.

Now all of us live together. I started a PR company and have been teaching Amber and Logan how to work with me.

And our mother is out of our lives for good after what she did to Amber.

I take a seat in the lawn chair, still holding onto the envelope. I lift it to my nose and take a deep breath, smelling the hints of his cologne that always seem to rub off onto the envelope reminding me of everything I'm giving up, by giving up Carter.

———

I feel his lips on mine and my body immediately wakes up. I open my eyes and stretch, loving waking up to him in San Fransisco.

"I could get used to this," I say wrapping my arms around his neck and pulling him into another kiss.

"I brought you breakfast," he says.

I bite my lip. "What if I want you for breakfast?"

He grins and pushes my arms above my head. "I figured you would say that."

"What are you going to do about it?" I tease.

He reaches to the nightstand where I see he's made eggs, toast, and bacon. Suddenly, my stomach growls at the sight of food.

Carter grabs something next to the plate that I don't realize is a tie until he ties my arms above my head and then to the headboard.

"Carter, I don't think I can handle being tied up," I say, my voice nervous.

He grins. "I know. You like control too much. But sometimes, this is what you need."

He grabs the hem of my tank top and lifts it up, but not all the way over my head. Instead, he lifts it just high enough until it is covering my head.

"Carter, I can't see."

His lips come down on mine and he kisses me gently.

"I know," he says again.

His lips trail down my chest sending chills all over my body. He's kissed me like this before, but I've never felt such intensity. My arms squirm over my head and my breathing picks up. I love it and hate it at the same time. I don't want him to stop, but I really want him to untie me and uncover my eyes.

"Just focus on your breathing Victoria. You can do this."

I take a deep breath in and out and then I feel his lips back on me again. And I forget about breathing. I forget about anything but him.

He pushes my legs apart as his cock rests between my legs. His lips and tongue continue to kiss me and I can't breathe. I need air. He needs to remember that I need to breathe.

My arms pull hard at the tie, but I can't get my arms free. My body squirms beneath his, trying to remind him to let me breathe.

His lips finally leave mine, and I take in a gasp.

"Do you trust me Victoria?" he asks in my ear, his breath hot against my skin. "Because if you trust me, then you can relax. You can know that I will take care of you and I'm not going to do anything to cause you pain. You can relax and let me fuck you."

He kisses my neck. "Do you trust me?"

"Yes," I breathe, even though I'm not sure I do. But I want to. Desperately. And maybe this is what I need in order to trust him.

One word and he owns my body. He kisses every inch of my body, making me squirm and feel electricity I've never felt before, even though he's kissed my entire body before. Somehow the blindfold and being unable to move my arms makes it that much more intense.

He pushes his cock hard at my entrance, begging me to let him in while he kisses my lips. It feels like he's asking me to open my heart as well. I'm not sure if I'm ready. Not after everything we've been through.

But as his cock pushes inside me, I know that I've let him far into my heart. I love him. I want him. I trust him.

Three things I've never thought I'd feel about Carter.

———

A tear rolls down my cheek thinking back to that morning. The sex was amazing, but he was equally as amazing afterward. He fed me breakfast bite by bite. He took care of me. And for once it felt good to be the one taken care of, instead of the one that has to take care of everyone else.

But it was all a lie. He didn't really care about me. He just wanted me to sleep with him. And he sure as hell didn't love me. He isn't capable of love.

I stare down at the envelope that I'm sure contains another napkin with another apology. His apologies are good. Seemingly heartfelt even. But they aren't enough. Not now after everything that has happened.

My life has changed, but I'm still the same person. I live my life taking care of my family. And even if I can find a way to forgive him, I won't forgive him for getting me fired and hurting my family. My family comes first. I can't forgive him for hurting them.

My heart wants to know that he's been thinking of me, but instead of opening the envelope, I don't.

I stand up and walk to the edge of the railing. I drop the envelope over the edge and let it fall slowly down to the pool beneath. It hits the water and I know there is no going back. It's soaking wet, even if I tried to recover it, there is no guarantee that I'd be able to read his words.

It feels right. It feels like after all these months, almost eight to be exact, that I'm finally over him. But the pain still remains.

He's ruined my life in so many ways. There is no way I will trust a man, not after him.

But I'm not done ruining his.

I pull my cell phone out of my pocket and I dial Lily's number like I often do every few weeks. I can check in on Carter and earn the paychecks that Lily still sends me by tweaking things to ensure that she stays on top of her game.

But this time, it's not just to benefit her, although it will. It's to benefit me as well. Because I need to see him truly pay for what he's done to me and my family. He's never going to stop paying for what he did.

18

CARTER

I'M TIRED.

So incredibly tired.

Being separated from Victoria has driven me mad. I can't keep doing this. Every day that goes by is like another needle getting shot into my body. And after almost eight months of getting stabbed over and over again, I just can't take it anymore.

I've been sending her almost daily napkins with apologies. I thought sending them would make me feel better, but they don't. They make me feel worse as I realize just how many things I've done to hurt her. I deserve to be in a lot more pain than I am in.

I thought she would respond. I thought that she would send me a text message. Send me a letter back. Even pass a message along through Logan.

But she hasn't. Not one single word. I can't handle not hearing from her. So even though I have four months left, I need to see her. Now.

"You're wearing that?" Lily asks, eyeing me out of the corner of her eye from where she sits getting her hair and makeup done for another show tonight. This one is on Phoebe's show again.

I look down at my jeans and buttoned down shirt, the same thing I always wear when we go on television. "Yes."

She sighs. "You need to wear something more dressy. This is the last month before the election and I need you to look your best. Go put a suit on. The grey one with the turquoise tie."

I don't argue with her. I've found that it isn't worth it. I just do what she says, whether I agree with it or not. At this point, I hope she loses the election, that way I don't have to stay with her longer than another month.

I walk down the hallway to the small dressing room, where I find the suit that she wants me to wear, already hanging on the rack. I put it on, but something doesn't feel right. It doesn't make sense why she would want me so dressed up unless something special was happening tonight.

I get an uneasy feeling in my stomach. Lily likes to spring things on me during the interview, that way I can't protest what she is saying. I just have to go along with it as true.

Lily is happier than usual. She's far too excited about our interview. Something's up. I just hope I can figure it out before she tells some other ridiculous lie about our relationship.

———

Lily slips her hand into mine. I fight the urge to pull my hand out of hers. I still haven't figured out what she's planning for the interview, but honestly, I'm not sure I care. Whatever it is, I'll smile and go along with it. I only have a few months left and then I'm gone anyway. There is nothing she can do to hurt me anymore.

We are announced and then we walk out, hand in hand, to the couch where we will be interviewed.

I smile and pretend I'm the happiest man in the world, even though I'm the most miserable one. I've gotten pretty good at faking it though. That, or no one really wants to look past what I display on the surface.

We take a seat, still holding hands. Phoebe starts asking us questions and I let Lily do most of the talking as usual. I'm just here as arm candy. I'm just here to make Lily look better.

"So you two have more big news to announce? Is it wedding plans?" Phoebe asks excitedly.

"We haven't set an exact wedding date yet. I've always wanted a summer wedding so maybe June," Lily says, looking at me with a toothy smile.

I nod. Thank God she's not announcing that we are getting married next week. That would be a hard no for me. There is no way I'm marrying Lily.

"But we do have some exciting news to share," Lily says, rubbing her stomach.

No! I scream in my head. She is not going to pull this crap on me. I can't keep a happy face, I glare at her a little, trying to put a stop to this before it starts.

Lily grips my hand tighter to try and get me to stop.

"We're expecting!" Lily shouts.

"Oh my god! How exciting!" Phoebe says.

The crowd cheers and my scowl deepens.

Phoebe doesn't miss my change in expression. When the crowd stops she turns to me.

"Carter, you look less than excited about this news. Care to share your feelings about this development?"

The crowd falls silent.

I take a deep breath. "Don't get me wrong. I'm more than excited to be a father. I just thought we were going to wait a little while longer before we shared the news. It's still very early in her pregnancy and a lot could go wrong. I just wanted to share this special time with her in private."

"Aw, how sweet. Well, don't worry. I'm sure her pregnancy

will go perfectly and you two will have plenty of intimate time together."

I don't listen to the rest of the interview. I'm too frustrated to pay attention. I don't know how she came up with this hair-brained idea anyway. There is no way she can pull off a pregnancy. And what's going to happen when she is supposed to have given birth and there is no baby?

I look over behind the stage and I see her. Just for a split second. Victoria. She's here. This was her idea. She's trying to hurt me. Still.

She can continue to hurt me the rest of our lives if that's what she wants, but I would prefer for her to hurt me while being mine. Or at the very least talking to me again so that I can see that she is happy without me.

The second that the interview is over, I jump up off the couch and run, needing to talk to her again. I just need to hear that she is through with me, if that's what this is meant to be. I'm tired of playing games. If she still hates me, I need to hear it from her own lips.

When I get backstage though, I don't see her anywhere. As usual, she disappeared before I have a chance to talk to her. She ran. Again.

I run my hand through my hair and take a deep breath. I'm going to find her. This ends now.

"It was Victoria's idea, but I'm guessing you have already figured that out," Lily says from behind me.

I turn around glaring at her. "I'm done, Lily."

Her lips curl up into a sly smile. "No, you aren't. We are just getting started."

"No, I quit."

"You can't."

"I just did."

She shakes her head and places her hand on my chest. I grab it and remove it.

"You're mine, remember? If you want me to keep paying you and Victoria, you will do exactly as I say. I'll ruin your careers if you leave."

I smirk. "I have a feeling Victoria negotiated her own contract that doesn't include me behaving."

Lily narrows her eyes and her smile falls. I know I'm right about Victoria.

"You'll never work as a fixer again."

"I don't plan on fixing anyone's problems other than Victoria's ever again."

"It's too late. If you leave now, everyone will just think you're running out on this baby."

"No, because there is no baby Lily. You'll tell them you miscarried and the pain was too much for our relationship. We couldn't stay together. You might actually get some sympathy votes."

I turn and walk away not caring if she follows the miscarriage plan or not. I don't care if every person on the planet thinks I walked out on a baby that doesn't even exist. And if the baby does exist, it's definitely not mine. The only person I care about is Victoria.

"She doesn't love you," Lily says, trying to get one last punch in before I go. "That's why she came up with this plan. To send a message that she hates you. That she wants you out of her life. She wants you with me."

I hesitate for just a second. Lily's right. I'm sure that Victoria hates me. But we've hated each other before, and somehow also loved each other. The hate can still be there, I just hope the love isn't gone.

I walk out of the building and straight to the bar that I found her in last time, eight months ago.

I look into the window and find her sitting in a booth, her back to me.

I smile and take a deep breath. She may hate me, but she wanted me to find her. She wanted me to fight for her. So here I am.

I walk into the bar and take a seat across from her at the booth. The table is high, and she leans on her folded arms that rest on the table. She looks different when she looks at me. Her eyes glow brightly. I can't read her emotions, whether that's a happy or sad look. Of anger or joy. I can't make sense of her expression.

"I missed you, Victoria."

She looks down at her hands. "I missed you, too."

My heart beats wildly at that. I still have a chance. But this is probably the last chance that I will ever get.

"Can I get you something to drink?" I ask, hoping that if I get her a drink, then maybe she will stay long enough for me to convince her that she still loves me.

She shakes her head.

I run my hand through my hair trying to figure out where to start, but there is no good place to start. So I start with the truth.

I place the engagement ring that I gave her months earlier onto the table in front of us. I watch her eyes look at it and I swear I see the desperation that she is fighting back. She wants to take back the ring, but something is holding her back.

"I'm sorry. Truly. If I could take it back, I would. I would take back every drop of pain I ever caused you. Every heartache. Every fear. Every anxiety. I would take it all away, but I can't."

I watch her suck in a breath as she continues fighting her real feelings.

"You should just go, Carter. There is nothing you can say that will make this any better. Just go."

"I can't. I can't just go. Not without you—or at least, not

without knowing I did everything I could to make it better."

I shake my head. "You got me fired. At least six times. How do you recover from that?"

"With love. Lots and lots of love. Because this is what our life would be like together. Maybe not at this extreme level, but we like fighting; you said so yourself. You like fighting and arguing. I do, too. And I like making it up to you. I've heard makeup sex is pretty good, too."

She scowls at me.

"Because you are my whole life. I quit my job today. I passed my company along to my number two, although I warned him that he would struggle to get a job as long as you were working. I'm giving up everything that I thought I ever wanted to have a chance at a life with you. I'll stay home and cook and clean for you while you go out and live your dreams. I'll take care of your family. I'll take care of you. I'll help you fix your life, like you fixed mine."

She doesn't breathe.

"I hope you've gotten all of my apologies, but I have two apologies left that I need to say in person. One, I need to apologize for making you think I was going to ask you to prom in high school and then asking Lily instead. I ended your relationship with Mark before it started and then prevented you from having a chance at another relationship by starting that nasty rumor. I'm so sorry. If I had listened to my heart, I would have taken you to prom instead of Lily. But I was scared. Lily was easy, she wasn't real love. But I knew that I could really love you.

"And two, I need to apologize for what I put your family through by getting you fired. They relied on you, and I hurt them. I've already apologized to them, but I will continue to apologize to them over and over again until I make it up to them."

She bites her lip and I know I'm starting to break through

her walls.

"How am I doing?"

"Pretty good," she says in almost a whisper.

I can't hold back any longer, I grab her hands and hold her as close to me as possible, while I lean over the table and kiss her. I expect her to pull away. Slap me maybe. Instead, she kisses me back. It's a desperate kiss full of hope and need. Our lips crash hard together and our tongues dance together like they've never been apart.

It feels right kissing her.

Slowly we stop, but we don't stop holding hands.

"I'm so sorry, Victoria. Please, let me spend the rest of my life attempting to make it up to you."

"I can't marry you."

My heart stops.

"I'm pregnant," she says and for the first time, I see the difference in her that I couldn't figure out before. Her breasts are larger, her face fuller, and I can finally see a bit of her belly protruding out as I glance over the table.

I wanted her to move on with her life while I was gone. I wanted her to be happy. She did that. And now, she's having another man's baby.

Anguish doesn't even begin to touch what I'm feeling. Sadness. Desperation. Depression. Disappointment. Fear. Guilt. Frustration. None of the words fully cover what I'm feeling.

Hurt. I'm beyond hurt.

"Congratulations," I finally say, because it's what I should say. I should be happy for her. I want to ask who the father is, but I can't get the words to leave my mouth. It is also clear now why she gave Lily the idea to pretend she was pregnant. Because she, herself, was pregnant.

I want to scream that this can't be happening. She can't have another man's baby. She should be having mine.

I grab the ring that is still lying on the table untouched and hold it out to her. "I want you Victoria. All of you. I want your family. Your baby. I want to spend the rest of my life loving you. I want to spend it taking care of you and your family. I would love to do it as your husband. But I'll take it as your friend. Or if you won't let me back into my life then just know that I will always be looking out for you. Even if it has to be from afar."

She stares down at the ring. "You hurt me, Carter. You're the only person who has truly been able to hurt me."

I watch the tears starting in her eyes. "I thought that by becoming heartless, like I thought you were, would make me feel better. I thought it would make me be able to protect my heart more and, in turn, my family. But sitting here now looking at you, my heart still hates you and loves you in equal parts."

"I'll take the hate, as long as I can take the love part too."

She wipes a tear off her cheek. "Can you forgive me?"

I raise an eyebrow and smile. "You don't have anything for me to forgive you for. I deserved everything that you dolled out to me in regards to Lily."

She shakes her head. "I'm not talking about Lily. I wasn't going to tell you the truth about the baby."

She rests her hand on her stomach that looks larger every time she moves. She must be pretty far along, which means she met the father quickly after we broke up.

"I don't deserve to know about the baby. You lived your life while I was picking up the pieces to mend mine."

She bites her lip and then the words fall out of her mouth. "The baby is yours."

I freeze. "What?"

"The baby is yours."

I jump out of the booth and over to her side climbing into the booth next to her. I get a better look at her stomach and realize that she is about to pop any day now.

"Can you forgive me? I wasn't going to tell you about the baby even though it's yours. I wasn't sure I could take the chance that you wouldn't hurt this baby too. But after I thought more about it, I knew you would never intentionally hurt this baby. I was hiding the baby from you to get back at you. I had turned heartless and wanted you to feel the pain that I felt."

I laugh. "I don't care. I'm just so happy that the baby is mine and not some other asshole's." I put my hand on her stomach, feeling the baby kick inside her. *Magical* is all I think as I feel the baby inside her.

"God, Victoria, I know I've made plenty of mistakes in the past, but know that I'm going to love this baby with everything I have."

"It's a boy," she says grinning.

"I'm going to love and protect our son with everything that I have."

She nods. "I know."

I hold out the ring to her, not sure where we go from here, except that I love her and I need to be a part of her life.

She takes the ring hesitantly in her hand, then places it on the ring finger of her right hand. "Maybe someday I'll move it to its proper place on my left hand, but for now I just want to be happy. I want to work hard. I want to take care of this new baby. And I want you to be a part of that."

I grin and kiss her long and slow.

"I know that you have mixed emotions toward me, but how do you feel about me right here in this moment? Do you still hate me or love me?"

"Why?" I ask.

"Because there is a restroom behind you that I would love to fuck you in."

She grins. "Love. Definitely love."

EPILOGUE

VICTORIA

I HEAR Charlie crying as I clasp my bracelet onto my wrist. We were supposed to leave five minutes ago for our dinner date, but it seems that Charlie really doesn't want us to go.

I walk out of my bedroom and head down the hallway toward Charlie's room. I guess our dinner date will have to wait a little longer. I make it almost to his room when Carter grabs my hand and pulls me into the hallway closet as he shuts the door behind us. He puts his hand over my mouth and makes a *shh* sound.

I raise an eyebrow at him and wait for him to remove his hand from my lips.

"What are you doing?" I ask.

"We aren't here remember. We are on our date. We haven't had a date since Charlie was born six months ago and we aren't going to get trapped here again. What is the benefit of living with your entire family if you don't take advantage of the free babysitting?"

"But Charlie—"

"Is fine."

I listen and I hear Amber and Sailor comforting Charlie down the hallway.

"See?"

I nod.

"You look sexy, by the way," Carter says, looking me up and down in a skin-tight red dress.

I bite my lip. "I thought you would like it."

"I'd like to see you out of it more."

He grabs the back of my neck and pulls me into a deep kiss. My arms fall around his neck as I breathe in his cologne. He smells good, almost as good as he tastes.

He pushes me hard against the closet wall and I let out a squeal.

His hand covers my mouth again. "You have to be quiet Victoria. I'm going to fuck you and you wouldn't want anyone to hear you."

"We can't," I whisper. "They are all just down the hallway."

"Then you better be very, very quiet."

He slides his hands up my thighs pushing my dress up until he reaches his goal. He hooks one finger under my panties and pulls them down, hard. He kisses me to keep me quiet as his fingers move to the slit between my legs.

"Carter," I moan.

"Shh," he says as he unzips his pants and pushes his cock against my stomach.

"Wait," I say.

He stops. "What? I'll make sure we don't miss our reservations, but I need you baby. Now."

I bite my lip. "I know."

"Then why are we waiting?"

He kisses my neck and I forget what I wanted to tell him.

I moan and he grins.

"God, I can't get enough of that sound."

He pushes his cock inside me hard and fast, while I wrap my legs around his waist and ride him hard. Sex with Carter is never normal. We rarely fuck in a bed and he always likes to keep things interesting. I sometimes pick a fight with him, just so we can have savage, rough sex that only he can give me. But right now, it's not about that. Because after seeing how Carter is with Charlie, I couldn't hate him.

"You want to come, don't you baby?"

I nod.

"Good, don't scream. Or I'm going to take you to our bedroom and really have my way with you and we will never make it to dinner."

I bite my lip as hard as I can as Carter fucks me into my orgasm. I try to keep my mouth quiet, but my whole body is screaming. My body tightens around his and my hands claw at his neck.

My orgasm finally stops and Carter grabs my left hand that is clawing at his neck far too hard.

"Jesus, Victoria. You don't understand how to be gentle, do you?"

I bite my lip. "Sorry."

He grins and then looks more closely at my left hand. His eyes widen when he finally realizes what I wanted to tell him.

"Does this mean what I think it means?" he asks, staring at my engagement ring that I finally put on my left hand.

I nod. "I want to marry you and have more babies with you and live happily ever after with you Carter."

He kisses me hard on the lips and I couldn't be happier. I never thought that I could be this happy. None of us did. Our lives started out so crappy. But somehow, we came back together and became a family, all under one roof taking care of each other.

"I'll marry you under one condition," he says.

I smirk. "Oh? I don't think you are in any position to be making demands."

"I think that's exactly where I am." He kisses me again and he knows I would give him anything.

"I'll marry you if you promise to never stop hating me as much as you love me. I'm not sure I could ever give up our rough, *love to hate you* sex sessions."

I grin. "I think I can give you that," I say, half lying. There is no way I can hate Carter, but pretending that I hate him is easy. I've had years of practice hating him. I'll spend eternity loving and hating him.

The End

FREE BOOKS

EllaMiles.com/freebooks

Want to get my full length romance *Not Sorry* for **free**?

Want to get my **free** bonus novella—*Aligned: Ever After?*

Want to know when I put my books on sale for **free or 99 cents**?

You can get all of the above and more goodies here:
EllaMiles.com/freebooks

198

ALSO BY ELLA MILES

Too Much

Aligned: The Complete Series

The Maybe Series

The Definitely Series

Not Sorry

Heart of a Thief

Heart of a Liar

Dirty Obsession

ABOUT THE AUTHOR

Ella Miles writes steamy romance with a twist. She's currently living her own happily ever after near the Rocky Mountains with her high school sweetheart husband. Her heart is also taken by her goofy four year old black lab that is scared of everything, including her own shadow.

Ella is a USA Today Bestselling author, author of the Amazon top 100 bestselling book: TOO MUCH, and Kindle Press author. She is also the author of the ALIGNED series, MAYBE series, DEFINITELY series, UNFORGIVABLE series, and NOT SORRY.

Stalk me at:
www.ellamiles.com
ella@ellamiles.com